The Ocotillo Review

Fiction Poetry Truth

The Ocotillo Review Volume 8.1

Attention Schools and businesses: For discounted prices on large orders please contact the publisher directly.

Kallisto Gaia Press Inc.
1801 E. 51st Street
Suite 365-246
Austin TX 78723
info@kallistogaiapress.org

ISBN: 978-1-952224-37-9

The Ocotillo Review

Volume 8.1

Winter 2024

Last Dance

Table of Contents

A Note From The Editor

Anne Lamott's *Bird by Bird: Some Instructions on Writing and Life* has been a big influence on my work, and my life, since the first time I read it (and all the times I've read it since). The title comes from the advice Lamott's father gave her brother who was overwhelmed by a school project and didn't know how to start. "Just take it bird by bird," he said.

This is the approach I've tried to keep in mind in accepting the challenge of editing and designing *The Ocotillo Review* while taking over the reins as Executive Director of Kallisto Gaia Press. The first is a creative process; the second, a largely managerial one concerned with balance sheets, progress reports, fundraising, and accounting. There have been more than a few times when *Bird by Bird* turned into something more akin to the Alfred Hitchcock movie *The Birds* for this right-brainer.

The saving grace has been my joy in working with our hardworking fiction, nonfiction, and poetry editors to read, sort, select, and edit the hundreds of submissions we get from our talented contributors. This is where the birds truly take flight.

I am in awe of the products of hard work and vision that came across our desks, and am proud to present our selections in this volume. But this will be the final issue of The Ocotillo Review. As many of you know, our founder and guiding light, Tony Burnett, has medical troubles which made it impossible for him to keep up the workload he had shouldered for more than eight years. This summer, I stepped in, hoping not only to keep the lights on, but to move forward into the next stage.

Unfortunately, that's not going to happen. Even as Kallisto Gaia suffered the slings and arrows of outrageous financial issues, I've found that the demands of my personal projects and passions leave me too little time to live up to the responsibilities of my dual role. It was a tough decision, but I can't let this organization suffer from my divided loyalties.

Kallisto Gaia Press will continue through 2024, publishing a lineup of award-winning poetry, novels, and short fiction collections. But *The Ocotillo Review* will not survive the loss of Tony. His vision and hard work gave us a wonderful run, but everyone involved in its publication has finally agreed that it's time to call it a day.

Sadly,

Mary

Sancho Panza's Last Dance

I return to avenge my friend in the shadow of a windmill.

Charging at it on my trusty steed, I cry a warrior's cry.

"*No hay viento en el infierno*!"

The windmill will not budge. It only turns. I pull back on the reins. My horse makes not a sound. There is no sound to make. It would be captured by the wind. My horse is not a horse. She is a giant caterpillar. She is not a butterfly, but her name is Luna.

Luna Panza, my only living friend.

All others are ghosts.

Ghosts that search the Heavens for my face.

"*Sigo vivo y no se porque.*"

What if I believe in the old dreams? The old fantasies?

What if I make myself a madman?

Will I then have a greater understanding within the space of memory?

Will I dance the old dances and sing the old songs?

Lyrics lost to me brought back? A tarantella? A paso doble?

What will my feet remember after my mind has forgotten?

I dismount from Luna and lay in the grass. The shadow of my foe covers me in topaz shade. It is not yet summer, but the sun is eager. She wants to burn me. She wants to send me to the dragons. I will charge them. I have nothing to fear.

Back when my friends were alive, I was the *voz de la razón*. I would shake my head and beg them to retire back to hearths where the blandest stews were boiling and the coolest ceviches were waiting to be consumed. I wanted to pray over my small blessings and keep those closest to me around the table.

"*Di gracias, di gracias. Porque seguramente soy bendecido.*"

The grass alerts my ears that ants are approaching. They see me as their windmill. I am an invader to them. They see only danger in my lounging form. What is safe when one is so small against the looming menace? Better to strike first and go to God later.

"*Lo siento. Estaba asustada.*"

In the background, I hear the sounds of nuns calling out for me. I am in their care now. One rainy night, a knock at the door and a plea for hospitable hearts. They are not permitted to tend to a man indefinitely. Indeed, they should have let me rot on their doorstep. Not a soul would have blamed them. They have their rules. Their order. The sister who plants and harvests the onions carried me in. She would hear nothing of the dangers of men.

"*Miralo,*" she said, "*Apenas es un hombre.*"

He's barely a man.

What do I give them for their trouble?

I run off.
I run away.
They search.
They find me.
I'm digging holes in the dirt.
I'm trying to find something that was never lost.
It takes four or five of them to drag me back to the convent.
I'm screaming.
Sweat pouring down the robes they've sewn for me.
Rope around my wrists to keep me in bed.
I'm a madman, but I'm not.
It's an act.
A performance.
I want to understand.
To understand one must occupy the space.
I scream as a madman would.
I rave as a madman would.
I talk of windmills.
The nuns pray.
I shake.
The sun sets.
Shadows cast me into dreams.
Lo siento, mi dio.
Lo siento a todos.
Lo siento.

And what have I to be sorry for?

Because I was a barrier when I should have been a passageway.
Because I was a naysayer when I should have been a champion.
Because when I rode alongside the brave, I closed my eyes.

The bravery knocked.
I would not let it in.

It was only towards the end that I saw the light of fantasy.

The moon parted the leaves of the trees and showed me the cyan truth.

As I clung to the familiar, I saw those I loved pressing on into the greatest of adventures. What danger there was relinquished itself at the foot of their bravado. I hid behind bushes. They did a flamenco by the fires of fear. They held out their hands. I only took it once mine was withered and wrinkled with age.

Aldonza loved me last, but best. A kind woman. She swore that after having lived to carry on the mantle of our beloved, she would pass the dream onto someone new. A young man with a few hairs on his chin barely resembling a bear.

She asked him if he believed in dragons.

He told her that he was raised by dragons.

She knighted him in our kitchen with a wooden spoon. A tap on each shoulder, and he was off to find the monsters of the world. He was off to tell them his name and the name that came before his and the name that came before that name and all the names that were written down on parchment that would be recoiled and remade and retold forever and ever.

Amen.

While she did this, I sat and ate my stew. She came to sit beside me. She told me she was leaving, and I would never find her, but she said that she would always live inside my heart. As a friend and fellow carrier of a shared story.

I stirred a few potatoes in a murky broth.
She kissed the top of my head.
And she was gone.

Dejó la puerta abierta al salir.

The chorus of nuns places my name in harmony. It becomes music. Sancho, a note. Panza, a word. I gather my strength to stand. Luna looks at me--   perplexed.

What is the old fool doing?

I begin to dance. I dance as the windmill cuts the sun and when the rays return I dance in those as well. I dance around the ants—careful not to crush my almost foes. I dance to raise up praise the way those who sing sing up the names of their dead. Their loved ones. To exorcize their grief. To say "No more."

No mas.

When the nuns find me, I am still dancing. A *paso doble.* A flamenco. I take the hands of the sister who looks after the onions, and I bring her into the dance. Her staid uniform flies from her body, and beneath it is a cebolla dress. We step on grass and it becomes floor. We look to the other sister and they have become musicians. We laugh at the windmill and the windmill turns into a dragon, but the dragon flies away.

"*Así es la vida*," the sister says to me, "*Fuiste perdonado antes de que nacieras*."

You were forgiven before you were born.

I take a step—not at something, but in longing.

A step in time.

Next to me, I hear a crack.

When I look down, Luna has shed her skin.

Now there is a thorax.
Now an abdomen.
Now wings.

She offers me her back for flight, but I decline.

I have not yet finished the dance.

- Kevin B

Machine Dreams

My driving journey began in the fields operating farm equipment as a boy. A boy who dreamed of Detroit machines as he used the hood ornament of his father's tractor to make clean, neat rows.

My body left the farm sturdy, fearless, unaware of the horrors beyond Colorado. In a world at war, I was born again of that madness. Landing on Omaha Beach, battling through to Cherbourg, and turning 21 during the Paris Liberation made love feel very far away. Love — the kind that occurred in the backseat of a Chevrolet. The Chevy Edy called "The Swamp Wagon." The Chevy that moved Edy and me along as I made the wrenching journey from hell to home. An uneven road for a young man who soon had his own young boy.

Once a GI, now a "G-man," the asphalt of a DC car lot scorches my government-issue rubber soul. I drive away in a '57 Pontiac. I've paid cash; to keep my feet on the ground before stomping the gas pedal, before motoring along Eisenhighways, before reaching out to the world to be kicked, then hugged, then kicked again.

Edy cannot have another child, and we must be okay with this. We are not okay with this — a baby boomless home. I can't tell my boy how much I love him; I can't say the words. I won't be able to for decades.

I correct my neighbor Ted: it's charcoal, not gray. An Oldsmobile Starfire, sparkling in the November sun, the 8-cylinder engine warming our behinds as the beers flush our faces. Young Ted is still driving a Chevy. I don't take comfort in his lot, just in mine. As I flick my Winston, I realize these are not Christian thoughts but squarely American.

A coupe works for us in a way that it can't for Ted, with all his tiny Teds, each as wonderfully simple as their father, with their watery eyes and doughy necks. My Edy looks on them — through the port-hole kitchen window — with a small measure of envy as she peels potatoes.

My boy is a hulk. He is going to college to play ball. To the groomed green fields of the Carolinas he will go. To battle other boys for position, for girls, for the manufactured glory that prosperity and peace have afforded. I am fine with it as he drives away in my Starfire; after all, an appointment with RJ Rowles Buick was made before his departure.

I polish my patent leathers in an attempt to blind the salesman, to impair his acuity and attention to the matters at hand, as we survey the Buick models. The final stretch of my working years, as I down-gear and prepare to leave the largest office building in the world for my basement woodshop. Retirement is an idea my coarse mother calls "fantasy." My father did not retire, she informs me, he died.

I drive the Skylark to the Pentagon in my late-career years, advising Kennedy, then, by tragic necessity, Johnson, then Nixon, to consider this and reconsider that based on gathered intelligence — but the trio steadily operated beyond facts. What began with idealism and domino theory paranoia migrated toward conventional warfare double-downs and an unfounded belief that what had failed for one administration would, for unexplained reasons, work for another. Over countless cigarettes, pots of coffee, and aerial maps, our team often craved a more defined enemy, like the fascists of our soldiering youth.

When I met the dealership owner's son, I was flanked by my own, now 60 himself. He and I used to take these schlubs to the cleaners, but now we couldn't be certain how we'd fare with all their computers, calculations, and lease options.

The Cadillac is silver. It is a star. A small salve for my widower wounds. It is also sad — the finality of moments like these — realizing the journey out-shines the destination. For it is a short cruise my Caddy and I will have together, just around the block in a motoring life.

I am no longer solid on the road. I now have what Edy would have called "incidents." Parked cars seem to be the key issue, with their penchant for jumping in front of my trophy sedan. Better to be grounded myself than by others, and that's what I do one overcast morning.

A title, a table, and two chairs accompany my grandson and me. The Cadillac of lore, the pot-o-gold, the finish line was to be his with a stroke of a J, a dash of a T, and the dot of an I. Having arrived in his Lexus, he cannot comprehend the magnitude of this; for I'm told that a Cadillac is no longer a Cadillac — how could that be?

He cannot fully understand the milestones and mile markers of the American road that I have traveled upon, that I still travel upon, now from the backseat of my Cadillac, the very top of the mythic Motor City Mountain.

- Jeff Stone

Ode to the Deer Mouse on The Basement Floor

"Hundreds of plant species are shifting their range, each following their own animal mediated trajectory." NY Times "Meet the Mice Who Make the Forest", 11/25/22

Your genius for self-preservation through
mutation could not keep you from this end
on the damp basement floor. Fur smudge.
Tiny bones desiccated to collagen dust.
Is it too late to consider the heroic life
you might have led deep in the Penobscot
Forest? Master mind of slow-motion relocation.
How industrious you might have been foraging
for acorns, gathering seeds too heavy for
the wind to carry, burying them in rich soil
where, forgotten, they sprout and help
the great oaks to migrate north?

Imagine penance and redemption as natural
as sleeping by day and foraging by night.
The weight of ill repute for your role as plague
host lifted from your flexible shoulders. Here
you would rest in your nest of grass and twigs,
hidden from the silent swoop of the great
horned owl, gently moldering into the forest
you helped birth.

- Elise Chadwick

Conversion Experience

Should I die in a forested dream,
may my papery words
be translated back into loblolly
or ponderosa pine.
Unspoken thoughts given voice
by wise-tongued ravens.
My knotted joints
rounded into skipping stones
to disrupt the icy logic of streams.
Veins twisted into vined milkweed,
to nourish monarch's ravenous children
as they prepare to transform
into clouds of orange flight.
May my soft flesh
knead itself with sand and clay
to become soil's honeyed manna.
And earth, air, fire, and water
celebrate the journey
as they transport my remains
to the place where all life begins.

- Jean Hackett

Why I'll Never Be a Butterfly

You don't have what it takes to become a butterfly,
the swallowtail sniffed as she sailed past.
No human could survive our liquid challenge,
when within the chrysalis's snug security, we surrender.
Let our bodies dissolve, atoms uncouple,
swirl inside a bath of transformation
until we awaken,
jaws exchanged for sipping straws,
hearts beating inside wings,
and nothing of our earthbound selves remaining
but memories.

- Jean Hackett

Carnival at the Next Village

Aunt Dini sewed gossamer wings for my birthday:
"Why don't you wear them for carnival?"
So here I am, tulle clipped on
my fur-rimmed puffer, whisked into the Citroen
to Catholic 's Heerenhoek, or "God's Corner,"
but now it's Paeregat, "Horse's Bum."
Whistles and nonsense schlager lyrics ring
in the blowing cold. We hop up and down
on the cobblestone, snatching glimpses of giant
monsters with papier mache heads, spitting
images of artists, athletes, and politicians.

During that week of reversed power structures,
tractor floats roll by a rich dish of satire.
Where I see Snow White and funny dwarves,
grownups stare at an economic bimbo.
Uncle Sam and that wine-stained Commie
grimly carve up a green-and-blue globe,
while I get distracted by dogs in business suits,
snapping at the bones of skipping skeletons.
Confetti and streamers spread an opaque mist
over sins committed for centuries or longer
and no one believes they can be changed.

While my wings double in the pushing throng,
I gawk at Prince Carnival in a harlequin suit,
who presides over the festival of fools,
accompanied by majorettes throwing up marbly legs.
Carousing constituents, silly with clapping, answer
his blue-and-gold scepter spurring them on.
The parade ends at the church square.
There, arms pump beer in bursting pubs.
The brass band nears with twisted trumpets.

I think, I can do whatever I want, too.
I work my wings into a loopy crown.

- Jacqueline Schaalje

On Prospect Avenue

Under the rush of the steaming shower, Javi sensed Mami pacing in the hallway, rattling the doorknob, shoulder pushing against the bathroom door. He imagined his mother's mouth at the narrow gap between the frame and the jamb, screaming, "I want my rings! *¡Carajo!* Javi! You have two days to clear out if I don't get those rings back today! Javier!"

Lately, Mami sounded like she meant business. But Javi had a plan. He had begged off from his morning shift as a short-order cook at Al's Café because today was Mami's eightieth birthday. He would get the damned wedding rings back for her this afternoon, cook her a delectable dinner later this evening, and tomorrow he would pack his duffle bag and be on his merry way, maybe head to Las Vegas where he had a distant cousin. He'd used up his welcome in the City. Even his sister Rita was turning against him. As for Mami, Mami was Mami, bless her heart. He'd given up any hopes of pleasing her a long time ago.

The shampoo bloomed under Javi's fingers and he silently thanked his lucky stars for the abundant head of hair he sported, blue-black and barely gray at the temples. When he opened his eyes two opalescent bubbles oozed down the glass door, and he made a wager as to which would hit the bottom first. As Javi happily scrubbed his belly, the bubble that was slightly smaller and surely faster than the other, burst. Jez-zus! He knew his mother's bad vibes had jinxed his luck.

It had been just a little over two weeks since the incident that had sparked Mami's latest unhappiness. Javi had bet his last check on Yoko Oh No, a sure-thing pony in the third race at Saratoga, winnings he had counted on to surprise Mami with a UHD TV for her upcoming birthday. Dejected by the loss, he rode the Muni to Golden Gate Park, a green oasis that comforted him whenever he was melancholy, which was more often than he cared to admit.

A boy hurtled past on a skateboard, and he wondered gloomily how Junior was. He missed his sweet nine-year-old who lived in Arizona with his mother. The gods—whoever they might be—had smiled on him the day Junior had arrived into this crazy world.

Javi claimed a vacant park bench near the Dutch Windmill, crossed his legs and inhaled fresh mown grass and mud. A portly man settled on an adjacent bench and began pitching cheese puffs from a bag onto the grass, creating a wide orange arc. Three bushy-tailed squirrels promptly materialized, then another five. Javi slipped on a pair of sunglasses and leaned back to observe the double-chinned stranger, who appeared to be in his late-forties, with a flamboyant scarlet Hawaiian shirt and a self-satisfied air. Javi was sure the man was a successful salesman on an all-expenses-paid vacation.

"Bee–you–tee–full day," the stranger sang out. He popped a cheese puff into his mouth. On his wrist, a Rolex gleamed in the sun with a dazzle of dials, the smallest whirring around non-stop. Javi had once owned a Rolex for five exhilarating minutes—a virtual lifetime in a game of Texas Hold'Em.

The man half-turned and held the bag out to Javi. "Care for a puff?"

Intrigued, Javi gave him a wide smile.

"So many squirrels," the man said.

Javi cupped his ear. "What's that?"

"The squirrels!" the man said louder.

Sensing something brewing, Javi lowered his sunglasses and viewed the man eye-to-eye. "What about them?"

"I wonder which of these tree rats will be the last to gather up dinner."

"I was just now wondering the same exact thing." More than a dozen squirrels had darted on to the grass, snatching cheese puffs before disappearing one by one into the brush.

"I'd put money on that gray one there," the man said, thrusting his chin.

Javi's blood quickened. A new TV for Mami was a distinct possibility after all. He kept his voice casual, his body relaxed, his focus sharpened. "They're all gray," he chuckled, quickly sizing up the remaining squirrels. "How much you talking?"

A half hour and many squirrels later the stranger drove Javi to Prospect Avenue and waited in his blue Mercedes while Javi borrowed Mami's wedding rings that she hid in her undie drawer whenever she went shopping. Ernie's Pawn Shop had been the next stop.

Javi stepped out of the shower and put his good ear against the bathroom door. Mami was gone. He danced a little mambo, invigorated. He was looking forward to cooking this evening. He wiped the steam from the mirror and inspected the laugh lines around his eyes. His chest looked out of focus like a person who never exercised, yet he liked the way he looked, devilish yet kindly, a man who enjoyed life, no matter what hand he'd been dealt.

Pulling on his customary black turtleneck and trousers, he resembled a cat, or better yet, a cat burglar, a suave ex-cat burglar, like Cary Grant in To Catch a Thief. Cary Grant was Mami's favorite Hollywood actor. Whenever he appeared on TCM, she'd make the sign of the cross and sigh, "*¡Válgame Díos!* Javi, elkarrrygrrrran and tu Papi looked like brothers, may they both rest in peace. They don't make men like that anymore."

When Javi and Rita were kids, Mami had taken them to see To Catch a Thief, showing in a Hitchcock retrospective at the New Mission Theater. In the theater, Mami couldn't stop talking, pointing out Grace Kelly, tan bella, and elkarrygrran, un principe, and those spectacular fireworks – blue and yellow and red Technicolor explosions over Monte Carlo. While Mami gushed, seven-year-old Javi was speeding along the edge of a rocky precipice overlooking the blue Mediterranean with Grace Kelly at the wheel of her sportscar, Cary Grant sweating and clutching his knees beside her. Pink high heels flooring the gas pedal, Grace serenely flirted with flying them all into oblivion, taking hairpin turns at maximum velocity, narrowly missing guardrails, angry pedestrians, protesting chickens. The scene gave Javi delicious shivers. Afterward, walking home with Mami and Rita on Mission Street, he found a silver dollar in a gutter, the silver glinting in the moonlight. From that night forward, he would always be anticipating the unexpected just around the corner.

Take his father Miguel, a man who looked like Gary Grant only in Mami's dreams. He was thick of chest and thick of thighs, with dark hair all over his body. A merchant seaman away from home for months at a time, Miguel had died unexpectedly from a spider bite in one of Macau's famous casinos when Javi was nine. Miguel had been the ship's cook, and by family accounts Javi had inherited his father's genius in the kitchen. Javi remembered little of Pops except that he had taught Javi how to make the best damn chimichurrí in the world. "*En esta vida, todos necesitamos un poco de buena suerte,*" he would whisper as he whisked and whisked. Miguel had made Javi promise not to reveal that luck was the secret ingredient. Crossing his heart, Javi was surprised and yet not at all surprised at his father's revelation.

Smiling at the memory, Javi slapped on cologne and was ready to greet the day. Mami was stretched out on the Louis XIV-style pink sofa watching Wheel of Fortune in a cerise satin robe, her dyed auburn hair in rollers. Barefoot, swollen ankles propped on a blue and gold Warriors cushion, she had the thermostat cranked to 80 degrees and the shades drawn. On the flickering TV, a perky blonde in gold spangles yanked on a giant wheel, sending it spinning. The camera closed in on the agitated contestants, who shrieked and clapped as the wheel whirled through random digits that could answer their wildest dreams. Recognizing the fever in their eyes, Javi watched, mesmerized.

Mami clicked the mute and turned to glare up at her son.

"I want my wedding rings back today. Javier! *¿M'oyes?*" she said tersely.

Javi tore his gaze from the wheel. "Have a little faith, Ma." He leaned down to kiss the air near her cheek. "That's exactly where I'm heading. I'll be back in time to make your birthday dinner. Rita and Tania and the kids are coming."

"While you're out there, St. Kevin's is looking for a full-time cook. God helps people who help themselves." Momentarily soothed, she pressed the remote.

"Every day is a new day, Mami," he said. "Every day, new possibilities." Javi spoke from experience. The incident that changed his life took place in the school's test kitchen the day before he graduated from the Culinary Academy many years ago. It had been an unlucky break, his lighting a match one second, a blast from the malfunctioning oven blowing out his left eardrum the next. He'd received a generous insurance settlement, but the long recuperation had cost him a promised position at a Michelin-starred restaurant. His prospects had evaporated. He eventually took a job making pancakes at Red's Café, filling in for the regular cook who was arrested after her mug appeared on America's Most Wanted for bank robbery, twenty-three years after the deed. Javi recognized that life was a crapshoot, and that was just the way it was. Too vain to wear a hearing aid on his right ear, he managed by reading lips and body language, skills that served him well at the card table, if not in sporadic stints as a fry cook in greasy spoon diners. Javi was a gifted cook, but the loud noises and the flaming grills in big kitchens made him antsy.

Javi headed to the pawnshop to get the rings. As he danced down the front steps, Rita was exiting the passenger side of a black and white squad car double-parked in front of the house. He loved his sister, but Rita in uniform wasn't a pleasant sight. Rita treated him like a kid, despite the fact that he was older by three years. She waited at the bottom step, legs planted wide, hands on belt, metal badge gleaming on her jacket. Her SFPD cap was set straight on her short black hair. No jaunty hat angles for no-nonsense Rita.

"Officer Krupke," Javi said with a crisp little salute, pushing past her. "You're early. Dinner's not till seven."

Rita caught Javi by the jacket sleeve, spinning him to a stop. "Big joker. What's that under your arm?"

Javi reared back and spoke loudly, holding his arms high in the air, the canvas bag dangling from one hand. "You wanna frisk me again?"

The day before yesterday, Javi had been trudging up Prospect with a pocketful of Lotto tickets and a bag of groceries when he spotted the new neighbor kid Maxie on his hands and knees next to his dad's yellow Land Rover parked on the street.

Maxie was shouting at tabby cat crouched underneath the vehicle. "Cumah, come here, girl!" Every time a car hurled by, the boy would shout louder, "Cumah! You're gonna get run over!"

The distressed boy reminded Javi of his own son. He joined Maxie by squatting and cooing, "Cumah, Cumah, heeere, girl," going from tire to tire and back again. "Don't worry, sonny," he said. He opened his grocery bag and bribed the cat with a generous slice of the expensive Italian guanciale he had bought from Avedano's to make bucatini all'Amatriciana. To Maxie's delight, Cumah emerged. The cat was cleaning her whiskers just as Maxie's father, Doctor Dave, rushed to the sidewalk, shouting "Hey! Hey you!" adding that he was tired of people stealing his roses. This to Javi, who for decades, had snipped red roses from that bush for Mami's kitchen table. The doctor went into tedious detail about private property rights and whointhehelldoyouthinkyouare-anyway? Javi took offense, mumbling whointhehelldoyouthinkYOUare-anyway? to Doctor Dave. He pulled out his Swiss Army pocketknife and began trimming his fingernails, deliberately shaving each nail, the steel blade catching the sun. Maxie, cradling the squirming Cumah, began to tear up.

"You're scaring my kid, asshole," Dave growled, knocking the pocketknife to the sidewalk. Javi was shoving Dave with both hands just as Rita had rolled by in the squad car, checking in on Mami during her lunch time. When Javi thought of how Rita had snapped the handcuffs on his wrists in front of the Doctor, Maxie, and the nosy neighbors peeking from behind blinds, his blood boiled. Only two days ago, Rita, his own sister, had cuffed, frisked, and stuffed him like a sardine into the back seat of the cruiser, only to release him at Mission Station after a totally unwarranted lecture.

Two days ago, and his blood still boiled. Rita was wrong.

"You wanna frisk me again?" Javi repeated now, still holding his arms high.

"Put your arms down, Javi." Rita raised her voice. "Watch my lips. I witnessed an assault while on duty."

"Taking a gentrifier's side against family. I see how it is."

Rita's partner leaned out of the driver's window of the patrol car and Rita made a slight toss with her head to indicate the situation was under control.

"Who do you think convinced Dave to not press charges?" she asked.

"I'm no criminal. I don't do drugs, not even grass, which is more that I can say for you, Miss High-and-Mighty, or maybe I should just call you Miss High, because don't think I can't smell the pot on you whenever you come by to so-call 'check on Mom.'" Javi used air quotes. "I could drop a dime on you, too, if I thought that anyone would give a damn. If Mami knew...but like I always say, family is family."

"She's not asking for any of the money you borrowed, Javi, just the wedding rings—you never should have taken them. They're all that she has left of Pops."

"Like I don't know that? Don't give up on me, Rita, I have a foolproof plan."

"Just bring back the rings, bro," Rita said and stepped aside.

"Don't forget—dinner at seven," Javi said. "I'm cooking something real special." The canvas bag tucked under his arm, Javi ambled down Prospect Avenue, which wasn't at all an avenue, just an ordinary residential street. He whistled "Lovely Rita", a Beatles song his sister always detested, and more so after joining the force. The sky was blue, the sun was shining, a bird on a telephone pole was warbling a springtime tune.

"Hey Javier—it's a great day for the race!" Ernie said. He meant the human race. It was his standard greeting to all who found their way into Ernie's Pawnshop, a quiet retreat from the tumult of Mission Street. An affable man, Ernie was witness to the highs and lows of his customers' fortunes. With his round body and bald head, he reminded Javi of a kindly friar, offering acceptance and financial succor to those who came bearing collateral at times of desperation.

A lanky young man with blond dreadlocks and a frayed backpack was leaning on the counter touting the virtues of his Fender guitar to no avail.

"It's a set rate," Ernie explained. "No reflection on this specific instrument, which I can see is a beauty as Fenders go."

Javi hung back, eyeing the familiar shelves stocked with forlorn saxophones and forgotten violins.

"Let I think upon it," the young man said with a Jamaican lilt. He motioned for Javi to go ahead.

Javi pulled a folded blue receipt from his wallet and handed it to Ernie, who keyed the receipt number into a computer.

"Five-one-two-three-seven. Diamond wedding set. Seven-hundred-fifty, plus nineteen days storage and handling, comes to eight-hundred and thirty-seven dollars. Make it an even eight-hundred," Ernie said with a flourish.

"Here's the situation." Javi hoisted the canvas bag on the counter. "I'm willing to trade my top-of-the-line set of professional kitchen knives—worth seven-hundred, probably more—plus one-hundred-sixty-seven cash—for the rings."

Ernie blinked at Javi as if baffled, then turned to the young man, who was listening to this exchange with open curiosity. "Made up your mind?" Ernie asked the young man.

"Ernie, I'm talking to you," Javi said, his voice deepening. "The knives are all I have. Today is Mami's eightieth birthday. I'm here to pick up her wedding rings."

Ernie matched Javi's voice. "Javi, it doesn't work that way."

The young man said, "I'm ready..."

"I'm talking now, kid," Javi said, eyes steady on Ernie. "Ernie, how long have we known each other?"

"It's business, Javier."

"I need those rings."

"I'll give you ninety bucks for the knives, in all generosity."

"They're Wusthof Tridents."

Ernie nodded to the young man, "Ready?"

The young man nodded and shot Javi a wan smile. Ernie strung a tag around the neck of the Fender while Javi wrapped up his knives.

"I wish you all good fortune, mon," the young man said to Javi.

"Didn't ask you," Javi muttered. He knew a phony when he saw one. He opened the door to Mission Street, and the sour screech of a car horn sounded in his good ear.

Mami was snoring fitfully in front of the blaring television. Javi closed the kitchen door, wrapped a white apron around his waist and filled a tumbler with ice and *Flor de Caña*. Dropping a wedge of lime into the glass, he took a princely swig, turned the radio to top volume, and swayed to Talking Head's "This Must Be the Place" while stripping the papery skins from cloves of garlic. "Hoooomme..." he sang and recalled his time at the Culinary Academy when he had been blissfully immersed in a world of creamy risottos and succulent sou vide quail. With another swallow of rum, he began mincing the garlic, shimming his shoulders, moving his hips, feeling the pounding rhythm inside his body. Time was all he needed to get those rings back, time plus un poquito de suerte which was definitely due him. None of them—Mami, Rita, his ex-wife—would ever understand the gambling wasn't about the payoff. Never was. It was all in the throw, the dice in transit, the brief singular beat when time stood still, the moment when nothing was decided and anything was possible. He knew all too well that the odds were with the house, but that spine-tingling feeling that enveloped his body and mind? He would never get enough.

Javi twirled to the vibrations, wiped his hands on a dishtowel and parted the curtains at the window overlooking the backyard. Where was the sun? Gusts of wind stirred the broad green leaves of the fig tree. Leaden clouds swarmed the sky. He predicted rain by five-thirty-five, give or take fifteen minutes. Javi laughed. He was in a groove, rinsing, chopping, and squeezing. He was singing to "Loco de Amor" and measuring olive oil when the pulsations in his bones abruptly stopped. Turning, he saw that Mami had hobbled into the kitchen and yanked the cord of the radio from the wall.

"Now what are you up to?" she said in a voice that grated on his good ear like metal against metal.

He paused and took a leisurely sip of rum before answering her. "Making chimichurrí, Mami," he said patiently. "I'm making some nice juicy t-bones and buttermilk mashed potatoes, topped off with a Meyer lemon tart for dessert. For your birthday."

She pulled the sash of her robe tighter as if girding herself for battle. "My birthday? What about my rings?" His mother never did have a sense of humor.

"How many times do I need to tell you? I'm working on the rings. You'll have them back tomorrow."

Mami scowled and tottered through the kitchen, gathering up tumblers, plates, and utensils and began thrusting them back into random drawers and cabinets. In her rising fury, she tossed his drink into the sink and the sweet smell of fermented sugar filled the kitchen. Even with bloated feet, she moved swiftly, and her voice pitched higher and higher, as she mouthed the words, "My rings, my rings," over and over again. The sound waves battered Javi's ear. He stood clutching a small bowl of olive oil and waited for his mother to settle down. Suddenly she seized the bowl from his hands and Javi yanked it back. Pale green liquid splattered the table and streamed onto the floor.

"*Ma, por favor! Vas a tener un infarto. ¡Cálmate!*" Sometimes he wished she would have a heart attack, she made him so goddamned furious. Jez-zus. He hated a messy kitchen. He swiped at the dark blotches on his pristine apron. "*¡Mira lo que hiciste!*" he shouted.

"You want to give me a present?" Mami grabbed a wooden spoon and slammed it on the table. Garlic cloves rolled from the cutting board and careened across the floor. "The best present you can give me is to move out and stop ruining my life. *¿Me entiendes?*" She screwed up her face and raised the wooden spoon as emphasis. "*Esta es mi casa,* you good for nothing! Your father, *que en paz descanse*, he would be ashamed of you!" She stepped back as if to swing the spoon at him and Javi instinctively put his hands up and pushed her.

He pushed her—not hard—and Mami lost her balance—maybe she slipped on the oil or the garlic, or both—and she went down like a prize fighter, hitting the back of her head on the counter. The pounding in his ear finally stopped.

Silence.

Javi bent down on one knee and scrutinized Mami's face.

"Mami?"

No movement. "Mami?"

Dammit all to hell. Mami just never knew when to let up, and this on her birthday. She was quiet, flushed cheeks fading, eyes closed like she was fast asleep, dreaming. Up close she smelled like lavender, pink mouth slightly ajar. She was too quiet.

"Mami?" Come on.

Javi's heart thumped inside his rib cage, shaking his insides, every beat like a sledge hammer. Oh god. What had he done? He glanced at the clock on the wall—it was getting late. He would bet that Mami's eyes would fly open and before too long her tongue would start working again. He gave her one, two minutes at the most.

Oh god. Javi rose up, kneeled again, stood up. Was that sound coming from the phone on the kitchen wall? He was having a hard time drawing breath. Where to focus? There was a lot to do before dinner. The steaks were marinating, but now he had to mince more garlic for the chimichurri, and he shouldn't forget the bitter arugula and purple basil for the salad, one of his glories, with green garlic chives, crumbled Roquefort and toasted walnuts, which thankfully he'd prepared yesterday, plus two or three just-picked orange nasturtiums from Mami's garden for color. He had to take the puff pastry from the freezer. Mami loved his lemon tart. He'd never forgotten the baking tips he'd learned from that pastry chef who liked to play blackjack—was Jacqueline her name?—keep the butter below fifty degrees and use a marble rolling pin. He would juice the Meyers just as soon as he cleaned up the shattered glass in the sink and wiped the oil from the floor.

The floor. Oh god. What had he done? "Mami?"

He couldn't think straight. Breathe slower. And focus. Focus. Should he call an ambulance?

Raindrops began to stain the windowpane. The ringing stopped. Javi dampened a dishtowel with cold water at the sink and was back on one knee at Mami's side. He gently moistened her pale face.

Javi squeezed his eyes to keep from crying and opened them. "Mami?" Mami hadn't moved. He was shivering and dripping sweat. He half rose to his feet, legs wobbly, his vision yellowed. He reached his hand out to find something solid to steady himself. Failing, he sat down hard on the floor. He drew his knees up and hugged them to stop trembling. Mami was his moon, always there for him. Even though they argued all the time, he loved her. He filled his lungs with oxygen and let it out slowly. It sounded like a moan. He got on all fours and brushed a wisp of hair from her forehead and caressed her cheek.

"Mami?" he whispered into her ear. He willed her to come to. "Ma?"

A flicker of Mami's eyelashes.

"Ma?" Another flicker. Javi's heart sputtered.

"*¡Carajo!*" Mami whispered weakly, getting up on one elbow. "Javier, help me up!"

A shudder of relief came over Javi. He wiped the happy tears swelling from his eyes and embraced Mami. Gripping her hands, he struggled to help her to her feet and to sit securely on a kitchen chair.

"How are you feeling?" he said softly. "Let me get you some water."

He watched as she slowly drank the water. His mother was a fierce tiger, she would be fine, her rosy color was already returning to her cheeks. Her eyes glowered at him, as if silently asking, What about my rings?

The telephone was ringing again. Javi glanced at the clock on the wall. "Rita and her family will be here soon," he said. "Stay here and watch me cook so I can keep an eye on you."

"Maybe," Mami said.

He fervently hoped Mami wouldn't mention her fall to Rita but asking her not to would guarantee she would.

Javi plugged in the radio and found a salsa show on KPOO. He began dancing about the kitchen. He poured a good amount of olive oil into a bowl and found a whisk in a kitchen drawer. "Did Pops ever tell you his secret to making chimichurri?" he asked Mami. The world was alive with possibilities. He felt a buzzing in the air, a tingle down his spine.

- Linda Lucero

Beachcombing

I have returned to that beach, where
    in other days you and I strolled back and forth
like the ebb and flow of surf on sand
    not knowing how much to cherish—

strode past calcified shells forsaken
    by the creatures they once sheltered
past dried algae and desiccated fish
    oblivious to the portent of their rotting smell

searched for small, oddly shaped glass shards
    we thought to treasure
their edges worn, their colors muted—
    each piece an elegy.

I tell you this because that shoreline has shifted.
    I no longer know how to move along it,
how to comb for delight, to live with desire.
    Yet I walk there now as if I could still step

in the same sandy impressions our feet made
    in those days we embraced
as if there were still two sets of tracks
    moving in the same direction

like other unbroken things—
    the limpet snug in its shell
the shore before the storm
    your soft and steady humming.

- Bonnie Wehle

On Edge

It's not heights that frighten me,
it's edges,
where the falls start—
too close to the canyon rim
where my mother,
always perched on the edge
of emotional collapse,
grabbed the back of my shirt,
held on as if grappling
with sanity itself.
I did the same to my children,
to my sanity.
Maybe it's genetic, this struggle.

Crouched atop a narrow
scaffold two stories up, I study
round cheeks—
a ceiling of painted cherubs,
wings of gold that need re-gilding.
On hands and knees
I squeeze the railing, viselike,
anxiety pricking at my palms.
The descent holds terror.
Don't look down, I tell myself.

I stare into the faces of the putti,
their puerile smiles seem more
like grimaces,
like challenges—
disguised disdain for the unnerved.
They have been here for decades
winged, yet fixed firmly in place,
and I, earth-weighted,
as stuck as they are.

- Bonnie Wehle

Requiem with Pinecones

And God said...let them have dominion...
over all the earth.. .Genesis 1:26 King James Version

The ground vibrated beneath my feet.
My skin waffled along my rib cage, rippled
up and down my arms and legs.

Over the engine's roar I felt
the trees shriek
shriek, as they were ripped from the earth.

A stand of conifers, where this spring
a hummingbird swooped
his mating ritual

and last winter wild turkeys gathered
ravaged
to make room for houses, sodded lawns.

An enormous machine yanked
thirty-foot pines from the soil
as if they were weeds pulled by a child.

Pine bodies stacked
like corpses of young soldiers—
a battlefield after the siege.

No taps were played. No bugle
no wind-stirred branches to whisper a dirge.

Was it you who questioned the cost
of such avarice to this erstwhile Eden?

Bulldozers are parading down main street.
Has anyone asked what dominion means?

- Bonnie Wehle

Donner Pass

Once upon a time in the long ago
stage acting was thrust upon me
at the tender age of ten

my having grown into the fifth grade's
annual communal tradition
of tableaux vivants and historical re-enactments.

Never my happy place,
public soloing,
piano recitals long raining torrents of torment

nor – I knew as past witness –
could proscenium or wings or vocal projection
provide cover for even a bit player.

During a manic part of the nineteenth century
in the wrong season on the wrong terrain
the Donner Party took a wrong turn into history

which itself took a skewed turn in the minds
of earnest teachers tangled up in notions of
period appropriate costumes and bringing the past to life

in the creaky wooden-seated auditorium
of the hundred-year-old bell-towered brick grammar school
still standing with architectural defiance in the later twentieth century.

The contradictions of the concept lost on the adults
the grand guignol aspect lost on none of the students
(although we did not know that term then)

there was thus much mustering of resources and enthusiasms
much whirring of parental sewing machines, not so much
of hammer hitting nail and wood, set design being minimalist,

so that verisimilitude became interpretive
with clothing wandering like Donners
somewhere between colonial and pioneer.

But oh the seams were straight and the cotton calicoed
and duly if inaccurately attired with a mobcap atop my head
fretful feet frozen to the floorboards

snowbound
within a script
no one knew who had written

I had one line
one spoken line
practiced desperately over and over

and uttered just before the curtain fell
on the first act, my last, my only act:
"Everything is going to be all right."

- E.D. Lloyd-Kimbrel

Jump

A majestic butte lies on the horizon.
Red-winged birds glide past.
Prairie rattlesnakes lurk close by.

Beyond Little Prickly Pear Creek,
Black Angus graze, white flowers
and trees jut from rocky hills,
waterfalls unearthed by Lewis and Clark flow.

Hailstones rain down at the buffalo jump
near Great Falls where in a ruse of nature,
young runners, draped in calves' skins,

once lured bison to the edge of a deadly cliff
by crying out in distress. Most boys survived.

The creatures' worshippers needed their remains
for tipis, food, clothes, and tools.
They excused the stampede … their lifeblood.

Drenched, we flee from the bluff to the bus
ignore the serpent warnings, prairie dog mounds,
find warmth and safety onboard.

- Amy Barone

Hearing Aids

Seedpod light, behind each ear
restored the assuring clunk
of a car door's closing
I loved the solidity
my father's series of black Wolseleys
the certainty of childhood things
within my parents' parentheses
I see them still
anticipate reactions
but I've lost their voices
know no aid
to capture that loss

- Ivo Drury

Death on All Sides

Growing up, contrary to my friends, I hated summer. While they used their free time to watch HBO and torture farm cats, summer for my older sister Maggie and I meant spending most of the day with our dad. He wasn't mean, exactly – not purposely. His vocabulary just didn't include the word optimism. The last thing he would always do before leaving the house at 2 p.m. for his maintenance job was give us a series of warnings to keep all doors and windows locked tight. From what he told us, the day we stepped foot out the door was sure to be the day we were kidnapped.

"You kids think these things don't happen, but they do," he told us one afternoon as we did the dishes. His eyes suddenly looking like he'd snuck in a line of cocaine while bending into the fridge to grab his bologna sandwich. "It happens every day to kids just like you. These kids, they're never seen again. Sometimes, they wind up dead, you know, in some ditch, or worse. What would you do if somebody kicked down this door when I wasn't here? Do you even have the slightest idea?"

There was an extremely long silence as his eyes bored into ours, as if the existence of these kidnappers was our fault, though my sister and I were only eleven and nine, respectively. "Let's see what you do. I'm gonna act like I'm breaking in. You try and stop me."

He went out, shutting the back door behind him. My sister and I just stood where we were, looking uneasily from the door to each other.

"It could have been a trick," I murmured. "He might be going in the front."

"No. He's still there," said Maggie, though her eyes darted to the front door. "I think I can hear him."

"Dad?" I called after another moment had passed. There was no answer.

Just as I took a step towards the front door to check if that was the way he was actually fake breaking into his own house, the kitchen door exploded open from a kick by my dad's boot. Even though he'd told us it was coming, I flinched so violently that my towel went flying. I seemed to black out momentarily, and when I came to, I found myself clinging to my sister's arm, which was pointing a large butcher knife at our father's heart.

"Well, that's what it'll be like. Only worse," said our dad, smirking. "You kids get ready. It wouldn't hurt to have some kind of plan in place for when they come."

With that, he locked the doors and pulled out of the driveway. After a minute of total silence but for the placid sounds of scrubbing and drying, I timidly said, "Should we make a plan?"

"Danny," she said, "just shut up. We're fine."

Our father didn't agree. After our sad display during his mock break-in, he apparently decided it was too late to save our lives, and opted to salvage our souls instead through daily Bible readings.

He focused most on Revelations, the Bible's last book, which details the imminent apocalypse. Beggars stricken by every malady ever invented and hounded by surreal beasts filled these father-child read-alongs, and my dad would always seem extremely disappointed when they had to end.

"This is all true, kids," he told us. "Every last word. Let me remind you what you read. There will be a thousand good years and a thousand bad years, and then God the Father will come down with his host of heavenly angels and God the Holy Ghost on his left hand and God the Son on his right hand. He will divide all people into the good and the wicked." He literally spat this last word out – as if merely referring to these sinners out loud left a putrid taste in his mouth.

It was a common feature of most of his speeches – there were a plethora of words he routinely spat instead of spoke, including, on occasion, my name. It was vicious – he'd cock his head back and all.

"It says that the wicked will burn in a fiery lake for all eternity. I firmly believe that we are in the middle of the thousand bad years right now." At this point he paused, as if to let us mull that over. The room was so quiet that we could hear birds singing and people laughing happily across the street. "So God could come at any time. He could come tonight. Nobody knows when he will come, and that's the point. If he comes and you're in the middle of doing evil, then He says you will die and if that happens to you, Megan, or you, Danny, you deserve it. That's right, Danny, you'll deserve it. So at all times, I want you kids to prepare your hearts for the Lord."

I spent that afternoon pounding my bed with my fists, begging God not to sort me into the bus bound for the lake of fire. "Oh, God. I'm so, so sorry. I'm bad. I'm the worst person," I whimpered viciously into my pillow, trying my hardest to convince God my tears were authentic.

When our mother came home, I rushed out to help her with the groceries. "You worked so hard, mom! I'll get these!" I cried, smiling so angelically I must have looked like a little demon. I gave her a huge hug, then seized all four of her brown paper bags.

"What the hell are you doing?" she called after me as I staggered toward the house. "You dropped one of them! If those eggs are broken, you're buying me new ones!"

That night passed without God coming, and so my concerns about Judgement Day faded along with my choir boy campaign. As I approached high school, my fear of my dad's many other warnings faded from my mind as well and were replaced instead with self-pity. All of my friends had fathers, too – why was mine the only one who had declared that watching Sabrina the Teenage Witch was a sin? Who made his children put on snow pants in October so we wouldn't freeze to death if we got lost in the backyard?

There didn't seem to be an area of life he couldn't put some cynical spin on. Investment, for instance. I heard his philosophy on the subject one night at the dinner table when I was 14. My mom had become interested in mutual funds after hearing about some of her acquaintances' handsome returns, but my father thought that was nothing short of fiscal suicide. Our money would be much better spent in something more practical, he declared.

"I seriously am considering stocking up on canned goods and moving underground," he said. He elaborated for my mother, claiming that, because of democrats, the world would go to hell very, very soon. "They want our guns, Peggy. They want our guns. I've been trying to find another way for years, but I – I just can't. I'm convinced the next time a democrat is president, it's gonna happen. Then it won't be long before we're all standing half-naked in soup lines."

Scowling, my mom just said, "Mike, we're eating." It was all she really could say. They had been married for over 15 years, and this was the point that she quit even pretending to listen to my dad's predictions of calamity, not to mention most of the other things that came out of his mouth.

"What was dad talking about?" I commented afterwards when he'd gone down to the basement.
"Pssshhhhhhffff," she said, shaking her head in disgust. "He doesn't even know."

After my mother stopped speaking to him, more and more frequently he began seeking me out to fill the void. He would tell me he just needed a hand for a few minutes to sweep the garage, and before I knew it, he'd have me 50 miles away in the passenger seat of his truck, cursing my stupidity for not hiding when I heard him approaching my room earlier. This vehicle reeked of cigarettes. Even during the rare moments my dad wasn't smoking, the enduring odor seemed more than sufficient to give me cancer. I'd surreptitiously crack my window a centimeter and casually lean my head on it as if I was just resting, then, with the side of my mouth hidden from my dad, take rapid, desperate breaths for a wisp of clean air from the outside.
"Quit humpin' the window," he said one afternoon when he spotted me. "What do you think you're doing?"
"Smoking gives you cancer," I responded simply.
"That's your mother talking," he said. "I can't blame her really – she's brainwashed. She listens to the mainstream media, and the mainstream media ain't nothing but liars and democrats." He suddenly swerved – he was so bent on haranguing liberals that he'd been turned completely toward me, speaking an inch from my face, and hadn't noticed he had drifted into the oncoming traffic lane. "Whoops. Yeah, they're all democrats, Danny. All of 'em. And they want to take your freedom and mine. That's why everyone thinks cigarettes cause cancer. You gotta listen to the alternative media if you want the truth."
By alternative media, he meant Rush Limbaugh. Rush's riled up voice was ever-present in the truck. The contempt he could inflect into certain words was eerie: he sounded just like my dad. When I occasionally questioned something Rush said – "Didn't Clinton just do that because…?" – my father wouldn't specifically answer me, but instead launch into an unrelated Rush talking point.
"That's what democrats want you to think," he'd say. "And your teachers, who are nothing but libs, by the way."
"Mrs. Oakley and Mrs. Pantzlaff?" I asked. I attended a Lutheran

grade school near our home in the middle of nowhere, and I couldn't believe that even in the minds of these bedrock Christians such sinister ideas had taken hold.

"Most likely," my dad responded. "You know, it's why I wanted to homeschool you kids. I wanted to really teach you something. You know, about real history. But now..." he trailed off, ejecting copious amounts of cigarette smoke from his nose, "it's just too late."

During one of these Saturday afternoon drives, we were on a two-lane highway when he suddenly pulled over.

"You're gonna drive," he said.

I was numb with fear the first few minutes. Then it was exhilarating. I got the feeling that this was something I was born to do – until a semi drove past from the opposite direction, and my dad began giving me advice.

"Every time you pass another vehicle, you're two inches from death, Danny," he said. "Just remember that."

I did. From then on, each time a car approached, I slowed down to the speed of a tractor and veered so far to the shoulder that my right wheels sputtered in gravel.

"Don't do that either," my dad said, grabbing the wheel with his left hand and ripping us back onto the road. "Get too close and the ditch'll suck you right in. It's like a vacuum down there, and let me tell ya, you slam into the bottom of one of those things and you'll fly through the windshield so fast you'll be shittin' glass right outta the back of your ass. So what you're dealing with is death on all sides, Danny. Sometimes all you can do is pick the lesser of two evils. And grab the wheel with one hand. That's how men drive. Just rest your hand in your lap and – there you go. Stay alert now though. This fellow in the truck coming up here may be drunk, so say your prayers. He swerves into us and this could be our last ten seconds on earth."

By the time I hit high school, I had learned how to handle these little hair-raising comments and even his hell-and-brimstone lectures. I agreed to every word he said, pursing my lips and nodding with the utmost gravity while occasionally throwing in little phrases I thought would reassure him I was on his side. "Yeah, the America liberals want is so sad," I'd say. Or, "'Democrats.' Ha. That's an ironic word. I don't think they even believe in democracy."

"You're right, Danny," my dad would respond. "You're so right."

In reality, I was almost completely indifferent to all the evils he constantly warned were, like a dark shadow, slowly enveloping mankind. I masked my indifference as enthusiasm, correctly judging it a good way to dull any suspicions he had that I wasn't the goody-two-shoes I pretended to be when he was around. Then I proceeded to misbehave – misbehave, that is, by his standards – under the radar. For starters, there was Harry Potter. Like Sabrina, it was forbidden in our house – our dad assured our mother it was nothing short of a gateway drug to the real-world practice of witchcraft. But my sister had gotten me hooked, and half the time he was out of the house, I'd sit in my room with one of the books, rarely blinking, like I was looking at posters of half-naked women. I had those too, stashed all over my room – from female pro wrestlers in lingerie to Brittney Spears, the woman I secretly had developed detailed plans to marry.

When my father attempted to make large decisions about my life, though, my true colors couldn't help but be revealed. This happened for the first time when I was a high school freshman. My soccer team was going on a two-week trip to Sweden and Denmark to play in a tournament, but he rejected my attempt to go immediately. It didn't matter that most of my friends were going, nor that I had secured a part-time job to pay for the trip myself.

"You know, there's just too much bad stuff going on in those countries. Danny, they're socialists there. I just don't trust them," he said. At this point, he looked at the ground and shook his head, apparently on the verge of tears that the world had gotten so bad that he couldn't even let his son travel anymore. "Europe was once the home of Christianity, but now they've turned their backs on God. Things are awful there. It's nothing but drugs and sex and sin. I can't let you kids go there. I just love you too much."

My dad's description of Europe only made me more eager to go. I would never dare ask him twice, though, so I did what I always did when he said no: begged my mom to talk to him. Whereas I was terrified to breathe even a syllable of dissent in his presence, the tone she took with him astonished me. I always felt scared for her while I listened from the top of the stairs, fearing that any moment, he might finally have enough and turn on her. She never seemed to realize that

that kind of danger loomed in these arguments, though, and maybe it didn't. On a few occasions, she actually bullied him so badly that if it hadn't benefited me – which it did on this occasion, as she finally got him to scathingly tell me, "You want to go, then go!" – I would have told her to stop.

He responded the same way when he heard about my sister's plans to study abroad in Argentina for six months in college, telling her that the whole of South America was a known paradise for sex traffickers. She was sure to wind up in their clutches. When it came to our dad, though, Maggie seemed to be turning into our mom. He'd forbidden her to go, but she seemed to consider this nothing more than an interesting perspective. When she got on the plane in the Spring semester of junior year, she didn't even tell him. At lunch on Easter, when he asked when she'd be arriving and found out, he was furious. There was nothing he could do about it, though: he'd lost her, and all of us, long ago.

When Maggie arrived in Buenos Aires, she found the girls she lived with always walked together and rarely went out at night – many actually did warn her that kidnappings weren't infrequent. It wasn't the only time our dad's words had proved to have some basis in fact. But his extreme views had begun to swing our own, almost as a matter of principle, to the other extreme. My sister and I became naïve. We each would travel anywhere we wanted, to the point that it began infuriating even our mother. That it infuriated our dad even more was the only silver lining she found in our wanderlust.

Eventually, I moved to South Korea to teach English. I've lived here for over eight years. When any news about the North's saber rattling emerges, it drives my dad crazy. His worrying is what seems crazy to me – South Koreans know Kim Jong Un would only launch a nuclear missile if he didn't mind one being launched right back at him. My dad loves documentaries about history, though, especially the wars, and he frequently reminds me of what happened to the Americans stationed in the Philippines in World War II. "Those people thought nothing would ever happen too. The next thing they knew, they were getting marched into the jungle by the Japanese to be tortured and raped and murdered."

His hysteria reached an all-time high in the winter of 2018, when American cable news stations devoted hours at a time to blaring the top story that the North had shot a missile into the sea and had issued "incredibly real, strong threats." My dad wrote notes to my mom telling her I needed to buy a plane ticket home or be trapped in communist hell forever. When I did visit the United States, he practically screamed at me not to go back.

"Something's about to happen," he repeatedly claimed. I didn't find this very persuasive. It wasn't long ago that he had also forbidden my sister from going on a road trip to the Western United States because "something was about to happen" in California. He seemed more frustrated than usual about my going back to South Korea, though, and suggested I try learning how the world works, which was exactly what I thought he should do. He'd never even left the country, for God's sake: what did he know about it? When I was lugging my suitcase out of the house a few days later, my dad met me in the kitchen to say goodbye. I expected some words of encouragement – something like, "I love you," perhaps – but I have no idea why.

"Remember what I said," he told me, his cocaine eyes dialed up to an eleven. "Stay the hell out of Seoul. That will be the first place to go. If you see a nuclear blast, don't look – you'll get your eyeballs melted right out. God be with you."

My mom and I chuckled over this farewell on our way to the airport. When we arrived, as I towed my luggage toward the terminal, she called, "Have fun! Try something new. Maybe in Seoul!"

The truth is, though, as time has gone by, my worldview has become more like my dad's than I care to admit. I've run into too many people like him who are extremely wary of danger not to become wary myself. My friend's father, the owner of a roofing business in my hometown, claims it's only a matter of time before all the anger in America boils over.

"Texas is going to secede in the next decade. Mark my words," he told me sometime during the Obama years, shaking a cigar at me to indicate his seriousness. "They're not going to put up with these taxes much longer."

A college professor of mine one morning sat massaging his temple at the front of the class and said, "Some people think this country's gotten a bit too big for its britches," he said. "Nobody knows basic skills anymore like hunting and sewing. If a few key areas were to go down – the power grid, say – things could deteriorate fast."

Reading Cormac McCarthy's The Road pushed me over the edge into a state of full-on, permanent paranoia. I haven't become my dad. But it seems obvious to me that society's stability is more precarious than most want to believe. You can't trust every Tom, Dick, and Harry you run into on the street, either.

I consider the precautions I take modest. For the remote possibility that the North actually invades, keeping a bug-out bag handy. Should a menacing figure begin following me during the night, carrying a pocket knife. In case an apocalypse causes the country to plunge into a serf-populated hellscape, a list of potential shelters nearby various cities categorized according to the relative merits of their water sources, edible plant population, and amount of canned goods I've stashed on-site. You know, the essentials. I don't want to go overboard. I just want to be prepared, and I think the people I care about would do well to heed my good example. Which is why, sitting in the passenger seat of my girlfriend's car as she drove behind a gravel truck recently, I hissed, "Careful!"

"What?" she asked, suddenly tensed up to the point that she almost lost control of the wheel.

"Sorry. I'm pretty sure something just flew out of that truck," I said. "You just never know. A rock the size of our heads could fly out of there and boom. I've seen Final Destination. I've seen it. That's all I'm gonna say."

It's why I tried to get the word out about the United States' metastasizing debt by telling my friend Jay about it at a restaurant last winter.

"Nobody cares about it! I mean nobody. This is trillions of dollars. That's bigger than the GDP! And if the U.S. goes down, well, jeez," I said, violently ripping the meat off my chicken wing. "We are going to be at the mercy of China and Russia, and then…" I threw my hands up in the air, leaving the horrors that would ensue to Jay's imagination.

And it's why I have begun considering it my duty to tell the Korean students I teach to steer clear of a city in Korea called Suwon. "Did you hear about the Chinese organ thieves there?" I always tell them. Looking concerned, they shake their heads no.

"Yeah. About five years ago two kids – they were about your age, had their whole lives ahead of them – got kidnapped by Chinese organ traffickers. These kids were found dead in some abandoned building missing everything but their bones and skin. Everything was gone. Everything. Lungs. Kidneys. Even their eyes."

One at a time, I glare at each of them. Judging by their spooked expressions, my speech is hitting home, and I'm glad: this is all for their own good. Taking their eyeballs for granted – not to mention their lives – has been a huge mistake.

"What would you do," I ask them, "if you were walking home tonight and ran into a gang intent on beating you senseless and carving you up like a watermelon? Do you ever stop to think about it? Have you even prepared for it at all? You kids think these things don't happen, but they do."

- Danny Spatchek

The Auroras of Autumn, II

Someone made an attempt to settle here…
Four walls of rock remain, ruins,
Above the creek, with mud
Of local color, call it "adobe,"
Still chinking the stone.
Four o'clocks grow at the base
Of one wall--
We have had rain this summer.
The wind piles red sand in a corner.

Stone and local color compose
Signs of invisibility, as if
Whoever built this was
Almost certain of failure.

I visit the place often:
It tops a favorite fishing hole.
In winter, it is a cold wind
That fills what seems to be
A shrunken canyon,
And clouds gather
To sometimes etch
Snow on the ledges of the canyon walls.
I turn my collar,
And cast with hunched shoulders.

- Benjamin Green

Pueblo Bonito's Ghosts

shadow me through roofless rooms
that stare at the sun like lidless eyes.
I try to picture family life in this multi-storied

masterpiece—three centuries' labor
abandoned in haste, before masons laid
the first cornerstone for Notre Dame's cathedral.

My fingers trace stonework as varied
as medieval tapestries, every panel
embroidered by a different pair of hands.

Did masons compete to create the most pleasing
designs? A Park Ranger says walls were plastered
with adobe, each room decorated by its occupant.

Did five-year-olds scribble on bedroom walls?
Did parents record growing children's heights
beside doorways? On the dirt floor, a stone-age

kitchen appliance—a metate to grind corn
for making tortillas. The Ranger squints when I say
I grew up eating corn tortillas—hand-ground,

with calabacitas, black beans and rice. I describe my struggles
to pat out balls of maza* —show him my uneven hands,
one stunted, ring-finger and pinkie frozen shut.

Factory-made tortillas don't taste as good,
but I eat what I can get, flip them on the comal **
with heat-seasoned fingers.

Forehead pressed against stone as warm as skin,
I feel—nothing. Pueblo Bonito's ghosts
have left me to fill in the gaps.

* *maza: dough* ** *comal: griddle to cook tortillas*

- Johanna DeMay

Composition With Large Blue Plane, Red, Black, Yellow, and Gray (1921)

1
Mondrian in his tight-
fitting suit, refused
            to return to the Netherlands,

to the tulip fields:
the square blues,
            long red rectangles,

black-bordered whites
and yellows brushed
            across rows of earthly canvas,

not until
it was legal
            to dance the Charleston,

its energetic jerky motions,
swinging arms, out-thrust legs,
            as if speed skating

across hardwood floors,
racing the music
            to beat

the clarinets, trombones, drums,
and the other thrashing couples
            across the finish line's

last measure
of evening.   Primary
            and clear–an illusion,

all the prettiness.

The borders between
spectrums integrated,

face to face, body to body,
hard color to hard color, then it was
all death's Boogie Woogie.

2

I was never a dancer
though my parents tried
sending me to the basement

of a private home
where chairs were lined
along opposite walls

there to learn to ask
someone as small
as myself for the pleasure

of stepping onto the dance
floor. I knew even then
it would come to little.

The awkward hesitation,
a swallowed stuttering
offer, sweaty palms,

arm around a warm waist,
held as if it were a broken wing,
feet entangled,

the snickering whispers,
a rhythm I could not locate,
a music smoky with

cigars and folded linens.
To outwait the hour

one-two-three,

one-two-three, not
the Charleston,
not the colorless ride home.

- Walter Bargen

Sometimes It's Just the Night

We could hear the storm coming long before we could see anything. At first, the thunder sounded distant and indistinct. A few patrons kept a close eye on the horizon. Most kept their eyes on their menus and their meals.

My attention was split between the approaching storm and my latest attempt at a story. Random passages pooled on the journal pages. I wanted a river. Nothing flowed. I could normally write anywhere, either blocking out external events or absorbing them and translating them into poetry or prose. Like a lot of writers, I viewed the world through a series of filters.

The diner was nearly at capacity that evening, so I had plenty of fodder. The middle-aged woman with jet black hair pulled into a loose bun held with number two pencils forming a decorative V. The old man with his biblical beard and a makeshift cane that drove golf balls in a former life. The sullen young man in army boots, camo pants, and My Little Pony muscle shirt. The red-headed family playfully arguing over who would get the last bite of nachos. They gave me nothing.

"More coffee?" The waitress refilled my empty mug without waiting for a reply. She already knew the answer. The same answer I'd been giving all day.

I wanted more. I always wanted more.

She swished away, like the dregs of coffee still in the pot, without looking back. "Let me know if you need anything else," she said. She might have been talking to me or to the family clustered in the next booth.

After splashing a generous portion of cream into the steaming coffee, I leaned back and stretched my cramped muscles. The curve of my neck landed with practiced ease on the padding that lined the u-shaped booth, and my eyes closed with no conscious effort. My ears stayed on alert for any sound or snippet of conversation that might spark my brain into action.

Small towns are a mixed blessing. Short-term inspiration and delight for writers and tourists of all stripes. A clinging veil for those left behind and those who chose to stay.

Another boom, a little closer now, broke the frenetic chatter of patrons into temporary silence.

"Mind if I join you?"
I opened one eye and gradually zeroed it in on cotton candy lips set in a round face. Fluorescent lighting did little to dim her natural glow. Her eyes were hazel, like mine, but telegraphed a genuine smile unlike anything I'd managed in years.
"I don't mean to disturb you, but there aren't any open booths."
The other eye snapped open as I forced myself upright. My inner critic screamed No! even as my lips engaged. "Why not? Not like I'm making any headway here. Slide on in."
She'd barely settled in when she flung both arms across the table and splayed her fingers as if inviting me to play Chicken with the steak knife. "So what are you working on? Is it a love story? A sad story? Does somebody die in the end?"
"That's all been done before. Sometimes by me. I'm trying to come up with something different this time."
"So you won't be starting with a dark and stormy night?" She flicked her eyes toward the painted picture window at the front of the diner. "Present circumstances notwithstanding."
"Dark and stormy doesn't have to represent some sort of bad omen. Sometimes it's just the night. Sometimes it's just thunder."
Her pink nails matched her pink lips. Only harder, less pliant. Or so I assumed. I had only my own lips for comparison.
"What are you afraid of?" she asked.
I looked up and saw myself reflected in her hazel eyes, little more than a shadow, barely a wisp. "You're not from around here, are you?"
"Just passing through." Her hands slid away and slipped off the edge of the table to rest in her lap. "There's always somewhere else to be."
I took a long, deep breath. When I exhaled, words spilled out, like a story finally starting to write itself. "This was supposed to be our somewhere else."
She tilted her head and said nothing.
"He moved on without me. Or I stayed without him. I can't remember anymore."
She smiled, the left corner of her mouth slightly outpacing the right. "Is this still where you want to be? Or do you want more?"
"I always want more."
Her smile broadened, and she extended one arm across the divide,

hand flat, fingers tight, and thumb pointed up. "I'm Tillie, by the way."

"Rebecca." I reached back and clasped her hand. "Becky." Her nails grazed my palm as we finally connected. I half expected a flash of lightning.

The lights went out instead. A few people yelped, more startled than afraid.

The fear was all mine, but only for a moment. Even in the dark, even as a litany of profanity arose from some unseen source, I could feel her glow. As I slid toward the curved back of the booth, I knew what I'd find there.

- Betty Dobson

Song of a Dying Man

Baby, it won't be long till I'll be tying on
My flyin' shoes, flyin' shoes
Till I'll be tying on my flyin' shoes
--Townes Van Zandt

Beside the Harpeth
your eyes shut to see
what could not be seen
above-ground
or on the surface of green water
a November day past
the battlefield
its columns of corpses
the buried
your ears attuned to
deep echoes
that sound
in the song
of a dying man
who would pray
for rain to pause
for seasons to linger
for winter
when light on the river
clarifies
silvers as a mirror
in which you appear
coming down
from the mountain
to help him rise
from bloody ooze
someone to tie on
his flyin' shoes.

- Karl Plank

Gravity and Grace

Well to live's to fly All low and high
--Townes Van Zandt
Maybe she just has to sing for the sake of the song
Who do I think I am to decide that she's wrong?
--Townes Van Zandt

To live's to fly
and to fall,
to fall over rails
from fourth-story balconies.
Not failing to leap
but to stay aloft.
With god-burned wings,
we dive.

A bystander might notice the form,
the tight tuck of a full-gainer's somersault,
and say "Well done, really well done."
Others are too busy to see
even the wild flair of limbs flailing.
It finally doesn't matter,
the points for style.
Too much grave there is
In gravity.

But also grace,
as one observed,
for those who do not break the fall
or flinch in the downdraft.
They fly upside down
to the bed-rim
of the deep,
listening
for lost music
of the drowned
listening
for the sake of the song.

- Karl Plank

Winter

Winter with its right dead leaves
And its dead live trees and its live
Dead grass and rambunctious dogs
Inside the dormant house with its
Children growing in spite of a sun
Mimicking an ocean-dawn moon
That stayed out too late, drunk, lost
In the vast sky, not knowing where
To glow or how to part the clouds.

Winter with its every morning
Is a slate, withholding a secret
Storm in its dusty belly,
With its rain that wants to be sleet,
That wants to be snow, that wants
To be ice returning unreadiness for
Future beholding. Winter with its
Squirrels tearing down to kitchens
Buried scratch-deep in the tramp.

Winter with its dried-up pens,
Can't write between grading,
Can't stand quiet cars passing
Knowing no one's going anywhere
Warm, with its wars, with its
Protests in the streets of Memphis
With its laws dressed appropriately
For beatdowns, with its mothers
Holding sons for dear life.

- Valerie A. Smith

From This Valley

From my window, I can see forever. That's what my dad says, anyway. It's not really forever, but I can see the sun glint off the roofs in Kingman and the ridges on the other side of the valley, all blues and greys. We are not quite on top of this mountain—sheltered a bit from the wind by being tucked into a little plateau on the Kingman side. Our yard looks like a museum to the high desert—flowering cholla and prickly pear, dug up from elsewhere, flower beds with volcanic rock borders and what would be wildflowers, old rusted horse shoes and cow skulls tacked up on the fence from when this was a ranch. I talk to the cow skulls.

My mother is in charge of décor. She cares how things look—to other people, I mean. I just care how they look. So she is always rampaging through the house telling me to pick up stuff. OK.

I tend to daydream a little, which bugs her. She doesn't daydream at all, at least not so as I can see. Maybe she daydreams about reupholstering the couches—I don't know.

I try to reconstruct this property as it might have been. I take the cactus out and put cedar and piñon pine back in—a few real pines on higher ground. I scatter the volcanic rock around the yard. I take the house out and see the contours of the mountain. Then I try to see who would have been here. Not cowboys—this mountain is too steep and rocky, and nothing that would feed cattle grows here naturally, so I can't see as how cowboys would be bringing them in from grazing. Deer maybe—we still see them in the early morning. Maybe rabbits.

I was really peeved when we moved up from town. I can't drive for two more years, so anytime I want to go to town, someone has to drive me in and pick me up. It's not like I had an impressive social life, but now everything has to be planned—I can't walk downtown and hope I run into someone at the Dairy Queen. And I'm stuck at school till 5 PM, when my mom is off work. I've turned into one of those people who goes to the library even when they don't have detention. It's either the library or join clubs, ugh.

At least at the library, I can read books I'm not allowed to read at home. Even stuff assigned for school, like Catcher in the Rye, my mother will pull out of my hands. She'll make me take a note to the teacher, saying things like “This so-called literature is not in keeping with the values of our family.” It is totally embarrassing. So now I read it in the library, that and more. I am glad to know someone else is dubious about the state of things.

If I could, I'd stay in the library till my dad got done at work and I could ride home with him. He usually has clients after they get off work, so he doesn't get home till 7. “Clients” is what he calls them to their faces. “Prospects” is what he calls them at home—which would make him a prospector and them nuggets to be dug out of the ground. Luckily I didn't open my mouth about prospects the one day the library was closed and I got to wait in his office. I liked being there—he sat with them in the conference room, and I could hear his smooth voice bubbling out. I liked the smell of the office machines—the big clunky Xerox that always jammed, the answering machine you could hear the voices through. I heard my mother's voice, higher and narrower than it usually is, saying, “Dan, Dan, pick up, please Dan.” I didn't pick up, though.

I wanted to try out the computer, but my dad said he'd take me out and shoot me if I did. It would be cool if they had them at school. You can write to people far away and they get the message instantly. Which is amazing because it is so hard to get through to some people nearby. That day, we got home at 7 and she was fuming, even though he always gets home at 7 and dinner is always cold. I don't get it—she wanted this house; he got a deal on it because he knew the developer and agreed to sell his properties. She couldn't pay the mortgage without him—at least, that's what he said when they were fighting. So it means he doesn't get home till 7—and we always eat cold dinner.

When I turned 12, I tried to talk them into getting me a horse. Each one of these houses sits on five acres, and we could surely find somewhere flat on these acres to build a horse corral. She would be a sorrel mare, the color of my hair, and we would pick our way across the broken volcanic landscape until we hit the end of the development, where Conway still ran cattle and where cool water filled a cement trough. I would put my face in it while the mare put her nose in it. Once we ambled back, I would curry her, and the smell of her sweat would hold me through dinner and the things they muttered to each other through their teeth. My dad said a horse was not a pet. You didn't put out that kind of money for an animal that didn't earn its keep, he said.

Sometimes I like to walk down the driveway to the barnyard. It's still there, along with a cute corral they built after the old one got torn down. It's like they want this project to feel like it actually is a ranch, without any of the trouble. That's what Chrissy says, anyways. Chrissy lives in the old ranch house—the developer lets her live there in trade for always being on hand in case prospects drive up. It must be weird for her to have her old living room be an office, but she says it reminds her of home. She showed me pictures of how it used to be. Now it has nice little knotty pine paneling and is decorated with lamps made from dead cholla cactus. Little windmill replicas stand unsteadily on the shelves. Before, the walls were just painted particle board, the dining room the green of cooked broccoli.

It irritates my mom when I go see Chrissy. I don't know why. She mutters about "that old woman," even though she doesn't seem that old to me. Her mom was friends with Chrissy for a long time, but they had some kind of falling out. I can imagine why—Grandma had always been cranky and Chrissy is always nice. Chrissy's daughter couldn't have children because she had some kind of radiation thingy when she was a little girl. So Chrissy doesn't have grandchildren. I think she likes it when I visit. We talk about books and the olden days. She says there weren't books like I read when she was a girl. I like books with magic, ones where kids who seem kind of dorky and don't have friends turn out to have a rare talent that will save the kingdom. Somehow, it is always possible to save the kingdom. I am not allowed to read those books but Chrissy said she wouldn't tell my mom.

Sometimes I can get her talking about what this place was like before the houses were here. Her eyes go out of focus, and I can almost see what she sees—the bunkhouse, the windmill, the dark red barn.

Me and Chrissy were drinking iced tea, talking about what I might do after high school. My parents want me to go to the community college and study dental assisting. I could live at home, they said, and save money for when I get married. No way: all those mouths, all that spit. What I love—besides cactus, and you can't major in cactus—is books. I want to go to ASU and study English, but my dad said, "You—be an English teacher? You can't hardly spell." I told Chrissy about it, how I felt like a heifer in a chute, loaded up for market. Living at home, taking voc classes, getting married.

"How do you think you could make that happen?" Chrissy asked, looking at the window as if she wasn't really talking to me.

"I can't see it," I said. The cherry tree I could see out the window was budding up to bloom. "I mean, if they won't pay for me to go to ASU, I can't hardly."

"Mmm," said Chrissy, stirring her tea more than it needed to be.

"This one girl," I said, "she got a scholarship. To go to some college back East." I didn't want to go back East—it seemed like all snow and bankers. I saw some of them when they visited my dad's office from the head office. They looked like they were in disguise.

"A scholarship," Chrissy said.

"Yeah, but I'd have to work really hard." I thought about my days. I didn't do cheer or Glee Club or Junior Kiwanis. Only dorks were in theatre. If I joined the literary magazine, my mom might read what I wrote. "If I got one, could they stop me?"

"Hard to know," said Chrissy.

We both turned toward the sound of a truck with a bad muffler. "Is that Grandpa? What's he doing here?"

The truck landed in the barnyard, a shiny black Syclone—speaking of not being able to spell—in a cloud of dust. "Ding busted!" I could hear his boots on the walkway, one louder than the other, then the screen door opening. "Chrissy," he said, "When is Conway going to pave that barnyard? I just washed my dang truck."

"Hello, Chet," said Chrissy.

"Give your old grandpa a hug," he said, and I stood up to hug him, trying not to inhale. He smelled like Old Spice and whiskey. "What are you two women hatching up here?"

"Not much," I said. "Just talking about school."

"Not boys?" he said, elbowing me in the ribs. "Why, your grandma could have told you a thing or two." His mouth quirked the way it always did when he talked about Grandma. She had left him when Dad was four.

"I still miss her," said Chrissy. I remember Mom saying that Grandma had been fast when she was young. It didn't seem like Chrissy was ever fast.

"What brings you up here, Chet?" Chrissy asked.

"Oh, I got to check on my best girl," he said, elbowing me again. "I got a business proposition for her dad." I tried not to look at Chrissy—she knew where this went. Often enough I had fled to her house while Grandpa sermonized Mom and Dad, calling me out of my room now and then to agree that whatever it was, was a good idea. She could probably hear the screaming fights between Mom and Dad that followed, all the way down the mountain. I still remember the year I couldn't get school clothes because Dad had bought into one of Grandpa's schemes. One day me and Dad went out to the monument to Grandpa's folly, as Dad called it, miles and miles of creosote and cactus crisscrossed with jeep roads, power poles without wires, white street signs with the names of trees that would have had to be transplanted, shipped in—palm, eucalyptus. An occasional forlorn rusty Airstream on a lot, waiting for water.

"Some day all of this will be yours," Dad had said, "providing the bank doesn't take it back."

"What would I do with it?" I asked.

"Wait till some bigger fool than me buys it off you," he said, turning right on Cypress and left on Redwood Estates. "Or, you know, you could get a dowser in like Conway did, find the water."

"How come Grandpa didn't do that?"

"You may well ask," Dad said, chewing his lip. "That man could talk a frock off a priest."

They were the opposite of ghost towns, I always thought, the memory of neighborhoods never built. Where we lived now could have been one of these, had Conway not found water. It was a sore point with Chrissy, that she and Clay had to sell the ranch due to drought, with no way to keep the stock alive, but Conway had brought a dowser up before he made the offer—and not told them there was water to be had. Chrissy wouldn't say so, but Mom did. Conway had some kind of conscience, I overheard Mom say, which led him to offer Chrissy her own home back, her husband dead and her daughter in Reno.

"Don't run off when I talk with your mom and dad," Grandpa said. "You need to hear this idea. Maybe you want to put your college money into it. It'll come back to you ten-fold." He was gripping my upper arm.

"I don't have college money," I told him, hoping Grandpa couldn't put a lien on the scholarship I hadn't gotten yet.

"Sure you do. Your grandma left you something—she sure as shootin' didn't leave it to me. I'll ask your dad." I could almost hear the trap closing—one of those humane traps where the door closed behind the mouse when it walked in for food.

"Ride up with me, Nadine? You and Chrissy can talk about your women's business later."

I shrugged, hugged Chrissy. Her shoulders were so thin I could close my hand around them. I was always afraid that one day I'd walk down to see her and find her curled up in bed, tiny as a child, her body stiffening. "Thanks for the tea," I said.

Grandpa made a show of switching on the four-wheel drive to drive up the road to the house. It was steep but not that steep, and it was paved. I always held my breath, afraid he'd roll backward when he shifted gears. He bragged about having a manual transmission when them sissies, meaning Dad and his friends, had all switched to automatic, but in fact the corner of his brain that needed to govern the clutch seemed to have gone mushy. He always tells me he'll teach me to drive, but I've got to get Dad to teach me first. As he lurched into the driveway, I imagined Mom calling Dad in from the garage. No way was she going to be on the front lines dealing with Grandpa.

"LeeAnn, Dan," Grandpa said. "And Nadine." Mom had sent me for glasses of 7-up with lemon slices and the little cookies grandpa liked. I set them down on coasters. Mom didn't like it when the glasses sweat onto the table.

"What's up, Pops?" I could see Dad parceling out how much rope he was going to give Grandpa for this next scheme.

"Dan, you're in business in town. Where would you say Kingman's economy is going?" They always began with a quiz, Grandpa's presentations. You had to go along to get it over with. "Mining's played out—even the feldspar. Nobody can make a living ranching as long as this drought goes on—that's how Conway got the OK to develop these parcels and swap the federal land around. I don't need to tell you that. What's next, Dan? What are you and your people talking about?"

"Tech," Dad said, as if he had a pipe between his teeth.

"Tech?" Grandpa said, his voice half an octave higher than it had been. "Tech? You can't build an economy out of that." I could see Dad trying not to say "Silicon Valley." "You've got to have currency coming in, people coming in, people carrying it in their pockets."

"But, you ask"—no one had asked—"what are people going to come in for? Kingman is not exactly your tourist mecca. People are not going to drive across the desert from the Grand Canyon to go to the Andy Devine museum. No. We need a tourist attraction. And we—this family—is going to be in on the ground floor."

No one said anything. We knew the drill. Grandpa would spin a tale, and then the grownups would all argue.

"What Kingman needs," Grandpa said, "is a dude ranch. Wait—" he held up his hand, though no one had tried to interrupt him. "We have plenty of land—the Red River Valley acreage. We have out-of-work cowboys. We have some of the best horseflesh languishing in corrals around the county. We have ranchers desperate to sell some cattle. We build a cute ranch house on the best parcel, a barn like somethin' out of Arizona Highways, dark red with white trim. We build a bunkhouse for them cowboys who've been bunking in with their ex-wives. Everyone will thank us. And then we advertise for guests. They'll pay top dollar for some baked beans cooked over a branding fire. Why, Nadine here could have a summer job taking them out on the trails." Grandpa leaned back in his chair, rubbing his belly, then rolling a cigarette though he promised me he'd quit.

The silence rose up shimmering like the heat off the highway, creating those mirages I loved when I was a little girl.

"Well?" he said. "You can work on it in your time off, Dan. And LeeAnn here, she's the best cook in town—everyone knows it."

I could feel my mom starting to sizzle.

I could hear my dad's deep breath. "Pops," he said. "Pops, we can't raise the capital. The bank's breathing down my neck every month for the Red River Valley payments. There's no way they're gonna give us a loan for a new project."

"Why don't you put down Nadine's college money for surety money? No way no banker's gonna say no to that. I was telling Nadine in the truck—she'd make her money back and then some by the time she graduated. She could write her own ticket—go back East if she wanted."

I held my breath as long as I could. I looked at Mom. I looked at Dad.

"Pops," Dad said finally, looking at me. "We had to use Nadine's college money for the down payment on this place. I always figured we'd be able to replenish it once we sold some Red River Valley parcels. But they ain't goin' nowhere fast."

"Well, I'll be damned," Grandpa said. "Her grandma must be kickin' up some dust in that urn of hers. I sure as hell wish you had told me."

"What good would that have done?" Dad asked. "You were dead set on that Red River Valley project. You made believers out of all of us."

"I've got homework," I said, slipping out from my corner at the table. As the smallest one, I had to sit where both my elbows touched a wall. "Sorry, Grandpa."

"I got to steal a kiss," he said, but I was good at this and got away with just a streak of slobber on my cheek. Neither Mom nor Dad looked at me.

I wasn't lying. I had to write an AP English essay on how Jim was more free than Huck. It wasn't like I got to pick and choose; none of us did: The questions came in a packet for my teacher. Four more years of this. Three and a half.

After a few paragraphs of sandwich writing—topic sentence, supporting sentence, meaningful quote, explication—I heard Grandpa's truck chug out of the driveway and the whining grind of his clutch. Someday the sound of someone destroying his clutch would make me sad. The voices in the kitchen went on, a duet of accusation and apology, treble and bass. I knew that song well enough to sing it myself. Finally the percussion section: my Dad's boots walking across the hardwood floors to my door, a knock, and the squeak of the hinges. He sat down at the foot of my bed. I scrunched up in the corner, leaning into the wobbly headboard.

"I'll make it up to you somehow, honey," he said, twisting his hands in his lap.

"Thanks, Dad," I said. I couldn't see what good it would do to make him feel worse.

"Do you still want a horse? We could probably swing it."

I could feel him casting about for some way to fix things. "No, Dad. It's too late."

We sat in silence, prisoners awaiting an arraignment. "Dad," I said. "Down the road, I'm gonna need someone in my corner."

"I've got your back, sweetheart," he said. "I always will."
It's possible he didn't know that wasn't true.

- Roz Spafford

Deconstructing Derrida

Almost no one reads his books today,
largely hidden and unwritten.

Example: speaking without understanding
he pretended to learn Hebrew.

He himself felt a divided person,
half Narcissus, half Echo.

His ego often spoke
with a ventriloquist's voice.

One of us really was expelled from school;
just him, not me.

In his cinema verité,
every proposition's not quite true or false.

Does his mirror reflect the true man
or just another mirror?

You may steal my words for free—
they are only an echo of his.

If you bleed it will be my blood you see,
even if we don't dream the same dream.

Echo repeats without repeating,
like a duck quacking in his feathered ego.

- Michael Salcman

It Was Better Then

the sweet of summer peaches
        juice dribbling

the crack of a bat
        ball soaring

smooching in the closet
        noses knocking

and I am pulled under
        back to being three or seven or fourteen

while waves wash the shore
and seaweed stirs smoky shapes
        I sink deeper

into the solace of the past
        before a refractory heart, a stent

before creaky knees and mulish ankles
        barely a shuffle around the block

before sags and creases
        and cloth-covered mirrors

spending more and more time underwater
until I can no longer see
        the flash of sun

the scale tips, the past weighs
more than the now
        which is only a whisper

- Claire Scott

Warrior Woman Comes Out Fighting

warrior woman comes out fighting
with ashes on her face
with pure rhythm, delicate grace
with hair running in the wind

warrior woman comes out fighting
with shawl dancing over her body
with fire eyes, an arrow in her hand
raising it   raising it

warrior woman moves in the rain
in the motion of wind and sun

happiness is a warrior woman
not scared of her power

warrior woman with ashes
on her face
and the memories of her ancestors carried in her head
she is fearless

she is a journey,
a wave rushing on quick sand
she is a journey,
a heartbeat in her body,
a drum beat in her body
she is a journey
she comes out quickly
she comes out fighting
she comes out ready to do battle
not to be shut down

moving as the water rains her body
moving as the trees rush her
moving a journey on sand hill water

she is not afraid to voice her difference
to carry her weapons in the fast night

she is a journey
the quick moving wind
the sand rushing under her feet
the whipping sleet
the hard driving hail

she is a journey
dancing across the land
long hair falling at her back
moving with the motion of the wind and the rain
moving with the motion of her heart
a drum beat behind her
a heartbeat before her

not afraid of the wilderness in her eyes
the strength in her hands
she is a journey

- Dorothy Johnson-Laird

The Last Small Farmer

at noon
there are no shadows
and everything is
glinting
the ponds, the roof, the silver tooth
of an heirless farmer
squinting

his cattle
board a flatbed ark
black and white
their eyes
flicking flaccid pom-pom tails
to swat away the flies

he slumps
against the lee curve
of a silo
mallard green
picking paint chips
faded
as the coat of his machine

thinking of that
John Deere
upon the auction block
he rubs his eyes and scans the skies
just like the weather cock

into a foreclosed homestead
he goes
to find his wife
writing FRAGILE on a box
wrapping up
their life

- Yance Wyatt

Haptic Trampolines

I need to be certain. Rounding up
won't get me a flexible hose that won't kink,
which spoils the flow. Who cares? It's about
nothing important. Great wingspan wider
than death or odes to Imagination. I like
the flow of simple days and weeks and duties
to wife and child. What is more important
than knowing you're actually living with
some hopeful text in your phone, good
news with the promise of proof the world
is improving or isn't? Haptic trampolines
in your man cave - Chingón! Life is good.
Worries are good for the lazy and dry
sand for the content. The tech inclines us
to leave the world. Write your Senator.
Weigh the biomass of monks and recluses.
Nothing new, maybe, just maybe, virtual
worlds can't be spoiled and make us cooler.

- Lawrence Bridges

Investigation

Nov 24, 2015: SAN FRANCISCO (KRON) — A homeless woman stands dazed just after delivering a baby.

What about all this surprised her most,
The people in their coats, looking at her for once,
Her blood that flowed, staining concrete,
Or that something carried by her body was, wetly, alive?
Living in layers, does one lose the distinction
Between the weight of outside things
And what grows heavy within, as if
Each week, a stone drops silently into a well?
Weeks after, by herself again,
a sudden pain wakes her.
Was it a kind of gift,
this tenderness, like an echo?

- Jennifer Hu

Dutch Masters

I prefer these overcast days
gray sky, window glass, and concrete
melding into a seamless surface
suffused with milder light.
Days meant for wandering.
They remind me of
the Dutch masters
who studied
light and shadow
over green slopes
chilled by marsh air
and the clouds,
always those rolling clouds,
in landscape after landscape,
transcendent, restless.
I imagine the painter,
brush in hand, smock wrinkled
and soured by yesterday's sweat.
He's slumped in front of the easel,
striving to capture the shape of mist.
Did he wonder, as I wonder now,
meandering through our city streets,
which is more important:
a relentless fidelity to things passing,
or the nerve to invent their replacements?

- Jennifer Hu

To the spring breakers parasailing off the coast of Key West or the cigar barons sipping rum on the rooftop of Havana's Hotel Nacional, the red and white boat idling in the Straits of Florida would have seemed as teensy and toylike as a fisherman's bobber. Hidden behind their Oakleys and sweat-stained caps, the two-man crew dozed in the pink shade strained through the cockpit's red canopy. The boatswain's stubbled chin lolled until it pricked his chest and snapped to attention, waking him so that he woke the petty officer in turn.

"Looka there."

"Huh?" said the petty officer with a start. "I don't see anything."

"Listen up."

"I don't hear anything either."

"That's my point. No gulls." The boatswain reactivated the sonar, which displayed a slightly different trench topography each time the green wand revolved. "We're in the middle of nowhere. You let us drift off course again."

"Me?" the petty officer whined.

"You were on lookout, weren't you? Besides, I'm too damn old to stay awake all day." In an attempt to save face, the petty officer lifted the binoculars that he wore like a necklace and fingered the knob until the line between sky and sea, turquoise and teal, became apparent as opposed to implied. He spotted a black dot disappearing and reappearing amidst those rolling blue hills, not sharp enough to be a shark fin and too late in the season for a humpback sighting. He pitched the binoculars to the boatswain and pointed thereabouts.

"I'll be damned," said the boatswain. "I think you just popped your cherry."

"I did?"

"Sit tight, sweet cheeks."

The speedometer jumped to twenty RPMs and the speedboat skipped across the water like a side-armed stone. They cut the engine and coasted alongside a woman lying facedown on a flaccid innertube as though a mighty wave had dealt her a blow. So as not to take on too much sun or lose too much fluid, she was unseasonably dressed in baggy sweats, her bloated limbs draped over the tube's circumference, her belly plugged in the hole.

"Ma'am? Ma'am! Señora?"

The petty officer grabbed the lifesaver from its mount and lassoed it around her neck. Meanwhile the boatswain fetched a megaphone from the cockpit and spoke with what must've seemed in her far-gone state like the very voice of God.

"This is the US Coast Guard. Are, you, alive? If so, don't move. We're gonna tow you in."

On the boatswain's nod, the petty officer reeled in the braided nylon one arm's length at a time until the momentum took hold and she drifted the rest of the way, finally thumping up against the scummy hull. Seeing that he couldn't deadlift her from above, the petty officer tied a boy-scout knot to the rail, donned a neon life vest, and to keep it from capsizing, lowered his feet onto either side of the innertube as if balancing a scale. But without much tack to his footing, he struggled to hoist her up even with the boatswain trying to pull her aboard with a bearhug—a chore on account of her weight, to say nothing of her odor. The longer they labored, the less careful they were. A bump here, a bruise there, and they quit apologizing and treated her as cargo. Nothing more, nothing less.

Eventually she slid on deck like a bested tuna. The petty officer scaled the gunwale ladder and took a load off beside the boatswain, both of them briny and soaked, the elder in sweat, the youth in saltwater. Yet the daytime dried them out at once, their arm hairs rising as though the sun were a magnet, furry and flaxen against perennial tans.

"Talk about rode hard and put up wet," said the boatswain. "If she needs CPR, it's all you, rookie."

"Aloe is what she needs. Or else her skin'll start bubbling."

"Reckon they sell that in la república."

"We can't take her back in this condition," said the petty officer. "They'll just throw her in the tank. We've got to get her to a hospital, stat."

"Wet feet, dry feet. That's the policy. Not our fault she didn't make it to shore. Current is what it is."

"Rock paper scissors, then?" They each made a fist, gaveled it twice against a palm, and threw down. Again the nose rose and the aft dipped and the speedboat, swinging sharply stateside, sluiced a whirlpool into international waters.

They were forced to decelerate twice en route: first so they wouldn't get tangled up in the mangroves, and then so they wouldn't leave a wake through Key West Bight, where the ferries launched, rich kids swam with dolphins, and the snorkelers floated facedown like their bodies had been dumped off by the Miami mob. Prior to arriving they alerted the land unit, which was waiting at Whiting Street Pier by the time they tied off.

It took four coasties to haul the woman ashore, one per limb. They roused her with smelling salts and after gaining consent rubbed her down with Alocane. The bottle wasn't economy size, so they portioned it according to the severity of her burns, double coating not her nose and collarbone as is often the case, but the nape of her neck and soles of her feet.

"Didn't have the good sense to flip over once in a while," said the boatswain after being asked to step aside. "Wouldn't want this chica cooking your arepas." He stood with one foot on deck and the other on the dock as the land unit peeled off the woman's wet hoodie in exchange for a dry, double XL, USCG T-shirt.

"Her stomach's all swollen," said the petty officer. "You'd think she'd be starving, but it looks like she ate a blowfish."

"Probably is starving. Parched too. Belly that ballooned. That's the body hoarding the last of its water to keep from dehydrating. You ever seen them feed-the-children ads where the old white man puts potbelly African kids on his knee like Santa Claus?"

"I fast-forward through commercials," said the petty officer.

"Your generation's soft," said the boatswain.

The sun had half-sunk into the sea, letting down a drawbridge of light from here to Cuba. The woman, more lucid now, pointed back to the boat.

"Looka there. Already wanting to go home. Oh you will, my dear. Soon enough."

"I think she's pointing at us," said the petty officer; and indeed she was. Heeding the volume of her moans, he played a game of hot and cold until she thrilled at his nearness to her deflated innertube. Turning it upside down and inside out, he found what she was signaling for. Duct-taped to the inner seam of the tube's donut hole was a gallon Ziplock containing an astonishingly dry EnglishSpanish, SpanishEnglish dictionary and a translucent cast of Saran wrap. Within the cast was a bundle of Cohibas corded up like a dozen sticks of dynamite.

"You gotta give it to her," said the boatswain. "That's damn resourceful. Making her own little humidor."

"Why go to the trouble when she could've packed more food and water?"

"To buy us off is why. As currencies go, it beats the exchange rate of a peso."

The petty officer endeavored to rebundle the cigars without letting any of the leafing flake, but the boatswain was less delicate in snatching them up for inspection.

"Give 'em here." This order was issued by the ensign of the land unit. He'd moseyed over to complete his report and now beckoned with the hand not holding the clipboard.

"What're you gonna do with them?" the boatswain asked, one eyebrow hiked like a tiki hut. "Tag 'em or burn 'em?"

"Oh, I'll burn 'em alright," the ensign replied with an incriminating dimple.

"That there's contraband," said the boatswain.

The ensign rapped the clipboard against the heel of his palm. "Come on. It's 'bacco, not smack."

"And all this time," the boatswain said, "I thought you a stickler for the rules. Turns out you're not such a square."

"I'll cut a corner here and there—round it off a bit—if I get a whiff of a good Cuban." The ensign ran one under his nose. "Reminds me of home."

"Round it down, you mean?"

"What have we got here, a baker's dozen? We'll call it an even ten." The ensign turned leeward to light an illicit robusto before sliding one into either pocket of the boatswain's cargo shorts.

"Let me ask you something," said the boatswain, who was senior in age but not in rank. "What've you got against good ole Swisher Sweets, made right here in the US of A? Right here in Florida, matter fact."

"Sweet my foot." The ensign scoffed up a plume of blue chimney smoke. "In America, the soil's full of chemicals. In my country, it's full of sugar."

"Your country?" said the boatswain.

"I've got dual citizenship. My parents came over the right way."

"A real patriot, huh?"

The ensign made fishlips and blew a bitter wreath upon the boatswain, who fanned it away right along with the irksome gulls that had risen like topsoil in a tempest the moment the ensign had put something sausage-shaped in his mouth.

"Keep that up and I'll make the call."

"Go right ahead," said the ensign. "But you call customs on top of immigration, and we'll be here all night. What is it you always say? 'Re-port, de-port, and still make happy hour.'" The ensign glanced at the face of his phone. "Already half past five."

"You two can go," said the petty officer, still climbing the ladder and paying his dues. "I'll stick around to fill out the paperwork."

"You sure?" the boatswain asked with another tiki eye. "Alright then. Come find me when you finish. I'll be somewhere on Duval." He patted his pockets in search of his keys, but the first thing he felt were the smokes.

The petty officer couldn't bring himself to throw her in the cage. Once the land unit left, he let her sit beside him on the pier looking westward toward the Gulf and the Americas and the life she'd never have. The mercury had dropped right along with the sun. He took a wool fire blanket from the boat's emergency kit and lay it like a serape over her shoulders. They ran out of shared vocabulary within minutes but sat there sharing a more telling silence. A boy and a girl who might have been twins strolled out onto a strand between jetties, buckets in hand, to dig for burrowing crabs. They caught one, dropped it with a shriek, then changed their minds and used the buckets for construction. The little girl sat high and dry atop a pillowy pink drift while the boy plunked down in the surf that fizzed over his lap like spilt Coca-Cola. They chirped back and forth in Spanish.

The Cuban woman watched them wordlessly, and then she strode barefoot as a saint on hot coals over the sand still radiating the day's trapped heat. She spoke to the children in a language they understood, and when she returned to the pier and retook her seat beside the petty officer, she smiled at the sight of the boy and girl doing nothing whatsoever. Suddenly, they seemed satisfied, if not entranced, by the sea.

They were still on their best behavior when the transport arrived. The petty officer made calming gestures to show the woman she had nothing to fear, and when the immigration officers didn't handle her with kid gloves, he was quick to apologize on their behalf. They asked him the requisite questions for a transfer of custody, then slapped him with a sheaf of paperwork to be faxed back in. Then they snapped an unglamorous photo of her and opened the rear door of a paddy wagon packed like sardines with other balseros who'd washed up on other keys. She climbed in and, gazing back at the petty officer, removed a pearl of a pill from a modest locket around her neck—the only item they hadn't confiscated, for whatever reason. Maybe because it seemed purely sentimental, even corporeal, snug as it was between her varicose breasts.

The van was out of earshot before the petty officer could intervene, and the woman was just another pair of bloodshot eyes peering back at him from US 1. He was as independent a young man as any. If he weren't, he wouldn't have left home for the Coast Guard, wouldn't have left a landlocked state for the margins of the map where misfits clash and latitudes yield to leviathans. But in the absence of his partner and his charge, he found himself seeking the company of the spellbound siblings still peering out at the fathomless deep. He took a chance on their English.

"What did she say to you? The woman from earlier."

"Shut up," said the sister. "She said shut up and meet in the middle. Me and mi hermano were arguing about where to build our castles. Mine kept crumbling and his kept washing away. I thought he was too close to shore, and he thought I was too far."

"She said shut up and meet in the middle, but not yet," the brother added. "She said it won't matter if you build in the right place if you don't build at the right time. So we're waiting for a few minutes of slack-water when the moon turns the tide."

The siblings resumed their vigil, and the petty officer was left to dot his i's and cross his t's under the lamplight of that selfsame moon. If the captains of industry could build a seven-mile bridge from Little Duck to Knight's Key, was it so preposterous to think there might be enough cable and decking, pillars and stanchions, to pave a ninety-mile straightaway due south? Despite the moonrise casting Marathon and Islamorada in a light more like midday come storm season, there were no windows through which to appreciate the jasmine, hibiscus, and hot pink bursts of bougainvillea, nor the chili lights and Chinese lanterns of Coconut Grove once on the mainland. There was only the darkness of the bulkhead and the rumbling of the floorboard, the growling of stomachs and the sibilance of prayers, the sound of the wheels hiccupping at the seams of each bridge until the stop-and-go traffic stopped once and for all. Then the doors opened and the poor, tired, huddled masses crawled out to behold an eerily familiar cityscape that would have them believe, in their collective delirium from hunger, from heat, that they'd ridden clear across the Straits of Florida, all the way home to Havana.

They stayed on Duval until last call, then traded glass for plastic and joined the stumbling exodus in search of a swiggy bonfire. First they tried Whitehead Spit, but the horizon flashed with the heat lightning of too many iPhone cameras. Even at this late hour tourists were snapping Instagram pics of the grounded buoy that marked the southernmost point of the continental US. Plan B was Straw Hat Beach, but skinny-dippers had already turned the boardwalk into a catwalk. So they broke away from the pack and left the gingerbread cottages for a wasteland of clapboard shacks demolished by the gales of yesteryear. They followed the tumbledown pickets that pointed the way through a wreckage tourists might have mistaken for flotsam washed ashore, spooking wild roosters into low flight as they went.

Reaching Fort Zachary Taylor, they downed what was left of their roadies and hopped the fence but steered clear of the barracks in case the nightguard were ex-Navy, not that jurisdiction meant much on a retired base consigned to sunbathing and Civil War reenactments. They brushed aside the palm fringe that served as a windbreak to a beach that closed at five, then kicked off their flipflops and went to where the water washed up around their ankles, letting the silt slip through their toes as the ocean breathed in and out like one great pneumonic lung. Before them the world was black on black but strewn with twinkling silver as if the sky harbored as much treasure as the sea. What had been a clear day was now a clear night. So clear, they joked that they could see the lights of Havana, but they both knew it was just a dinner cruise coming in. Otherwise the evening was so empty, the vacuum so vast, they had to fill it with small talk just to maintain a sense of scale.

"Are you from here?" asked the petty officer. "I mean actually from here?"

"You're asking am I a goddamn Conch?" The boatswain was drunk on rum runners and inarticulate, now deploying expletives where adjectives should go. "I'm a fuckin' Kentuckian is what I am. American by birth, Southern by the grace of God."

"Wasn't Kentucky neutral?"

"Birthplace of bourbon and bluegrass. That's more than I can say for this place, no matter how far south we are."

"If you're that against it, why'd you put in to be stationed here?"

"Sleight of hand." The boatswain produced the two hidden robustos. He bit and spat, cupped a palm and chuffed both alight with the same slender flame, his face dawning and setting in the span of a struck match. "With the White House so focused on walling out the Mexicans, they're letting Cubans spill in olly olly oxen free. Tell me, what good is it locking the front door if you leave the back wide open?"

The petty officer plugged the robusto in his mouth as an excuse not to speak. All he contributed to the conversation was a prohibitive cough.

"Don't inhale her. Just taste." The boatswain drew a curling mouthful by way of example. "Alright, your turn. How's it you got all the way down here to the Florida Keys, dribble of America's dick?"

"I'll tell you when I figure it out myself," said the petty officer.

"You could use most people's excuse and say you were chasing a girl."

"More like the opposite."

"The girl chased you?"

"That's not what I meant by opposite. Back home I was a fish out of water. So one day, I jumped in my truck and drove down the coast till I ran out of real estate."

"And you never looked back," the boatswain presumed with a sage and squinty toke.

"I thought that's what we were doing now."

"Not from where I'm standing, partner. Seems to me you're looking straight ahead. New horizons and whatnot."

Whereas the boatswain's smoke rings had become a steady industry, the petty officer's unsmoked robusto paid out a thin ribbon as it transformed itself into ash like a wand of incense. "Then what I did, you wouldn't call it running away from home?"

"That'd be a hell of a note. Given your job is keeping folks from doing just that."

"I don't see it that way," said the petty officer. "The way I see it, we might be helping them just as soon as turning them back. I mean, what's Key West if not a welcoming party? Come one, come all."

"Spoken like a true lefty," said the boatswain.

On that note he called it a night. His Cuban was down to the knuckle anyhow. As he retreated up the coast into the curved and licking darkness, the flaring cherry became the port light of a vessel or the wingtip of a plane. The petty officer found himself alone again. No partner. No charge. No children building sandcastles. He checked that he had reception, then made the call he'd been putting off.

"Dade County Refugee Center."

"I'm a Petty Officer Third Class stationed down here in Key West, and I'm calling in regards to a woman we picked up in the Straits today. She didn't have ID on her, but she was wearing this locket. And the weird thing is, I saw her take something out of it and put it in her mouth right before she was hauled off to Miami for processing. I'm not asking for any specifics. I just want to make sure she's okay. That it wasn't, like, a kill-pill or something."

"She's alive alright. Rough shape, though. Third-degree burns on the neck and feet, and the mother of all yeast infections."

"You can share that information over the phone?"

"She's not entitled to privacy. Isn't a US citizen. Her son, on the other hand, is, so says the Fourteenth Amendment. Wet foot, dry foot."

"She has a son in the States?"

"In the infirmary. As of twenty minutes ago. They found the locket in her cleavage during a cavity search. Still had a few pills inside it. They thought she might be smuggling a soluble narcotic, so they sent it to the lab. Turns out it was Pitocin."

"Pitocin?"

"You know, the stuff that induces labor. Hello? Officer? Hello?"

The petty officer stood with the phone to his ear until realizing he'd been hung up on in response to his own gaping silence. The soundscape of the conversation gave way to the seascape before him and, with a tilt of the head, the celestial carousel up above. Were there really a man in the moon, he would have been grinning as coolly as the crayon sun in the corner of every family portrait ever drawn by a boy. Like the warm equatorial current of the same name, el niño had been born of two worlds and would forever have passage between them. The petty officer had been an unwitting but not unwilling doula to this deliverance.

"Huh." He dropped the filthy cigar with a hiss and followed his footprints home.

- Yance Wyatt

I have Some Questions for God
(An Abecedarian Poem)

Another day starts in this city of mine
beautiful tall trees are all around
chasing each other, two baby squirrels
dogs running around, joy in their eyes

Everybody seems so happy in this city
feather on the ground, the passage of time
girls are in the playground
hugging the colorful butterflies

In the sky two birds are singing a love song
just around the corner from us, in a park
kids are jumping in a fountain, up and down

Life is so beautiful in this city of mine
mountains in the background, tall and strong
nearby, a lake and a river, full of playful trout

Oh, I so much want to stop the passage of time,
pause to see the colors of the rainbow in the sky

Questions, I have many of them for God: How to
retain peace in this city of mine? How to keep
smell of roses and lavenders alive? How to
take care of so much beauty that I find around

Voice of God echoed in my mind, my son:
Wisdom is what you need, search for the truth
Exclude excesses that damage nature's balance
You will find peace with the genuine love of others
Zen is the path to reach God, practice it

- Hossein Hakim

The Last Status Symbol

When the world boils over
        the heat of our consumption,
imagine who will be wearing

        the last status symbol:
orbs of dew captured
        in glass, dangling

from the nape and lobe
        of the richest among us.
Instead of a Louis Vuitton,

        the Estelle's of our elite
will wear a plastic pouch
        of water, clean and clear!

It will swing sophisticated
        from a right elbow akimbo.
Embossed insignia repeating

        double H's and O's
will be the watermark
        for any thirsty among

us to read and weep from
        the purses of few: I have water.
I have water. I have it all!

- Jenny Maaketo

Grendel's Mother Considers Wells Beach, Maine

Imagine that, not wanting or needing a name. Each
droplet in the ocean cannot be summoned
but moves as one body does. Grendel's mother
floats, her girth turned to blubber to be carried.
She learned how to swim in the forest, in whirlpools
of leaf-rot and dirt. It's lighter out here, in the Atlantic,
drowsy and empty, sunbaked belly, sand-baked paws.

No one seems to notice her, the beachgoers all
one plant with umbrella blooms. So,
Grendel's mother swims by the beach, unafraid of
being hunted but afraid to really drift out there,
afraid to truly become lessmore. She is half-dissolved now, like
the moonlight on water—there but not.

She considers that the other swimmers don't go full
liquid either. A human mother a little too fat for
her modest two-piece dives headfirst
into the waves, mouth open for salt, seaweed,
and wild. Grendel's mother surmises the swimmer
is tired of filling herself with sweet things and takes
in what she can get. And yet, she too, doesn't give.
The human mother looks over her shoulder to her family
on the beach, pale husband, small child eating sand. Imagine that,
though, still having an anchor that's actual, thinks Grendel's mother,
imagine having someone calling you from the shore.
Imagine a reason to stay.

- Nadia Arioli

Grendel's Mother Considers the Bones You Cannot Touch

in the room of given light

in the museum where children go,

each in a line of linked bones

there is a colossus indelible

more real than dragons or other monsters

larger too the bones are for looking

but not touching. never touching

remote as any icon beast made saint

beast made sacred and like plovers

and infants all terrible mouth.

- Nadia Arioli

Grendel's Mother Considers the Sphinx Moth

I am trying to find a story in which an animal is written about fairly.

In Edgar Allan Poe's short story The Sphinx, the narrator is quarantined with his friend to try to weather a plague. It sounds familiar because it is. Death is ravaging the countryside, word arrives that their friends are dead. No longer just a fact, death is a force that's hard to explain but nonetheless true: like love, magnets, and God.

In this state, the narrator looks out of the window and sees a foul beast charging down the hillside, crushing the landscape with its terrible legs. The twist, of course—and these things always have a twist—is that the beast is merely a sphinx moth on a tendril in front of the window. It was a trick of forced perspective, like a photo your uncle might take of you holding up the Tower of Pisa.

The ending is that the beast isn't real, and all is well. Except, not really, because the terror at such a monster was real, the feeling of dread and like your losing your mind is real. The lesson is, don't let fear get the better of you. The lesson is, sometimes scary things are small, like a drop of blood carrying a plague, like a baby.

Several times a year, the female sphinx moth lays eggs, typically in a clutch, all on the same flower. Depending on the sub-species, the eggs take between three and twenty-one days to hatch. Like all butterflies and moths, the young are born as caterpillars, usually with five pairs of prolegs. Sometimes, a sub-species may have a horn on the end, which is why a sphinx moth can be known as a horned caterpillar.

(Strange that an infant can be so different than the parent. A wonder the moths can reproduce at all.)

(When he was born, I looked in his eyes and saw myself.)

The young hold themselves in a pushup-like pose and head facing forward, like a Sphinx at the great pyramid of Giza.

So, it's not about riddles. Tell me: What is bigger when it's far away?

The young are camouflaged. To have quiet children who are nothing like you.

Then the caterpillars do what caterpillars do, namely transform into moths, and that is beautiful and profound and not at all like a beast-mother terrorizing down a hill. The imaginal cells turn to goo, and the full moth emerges. The mothers are gone by that point, but the cells know—hardcoded into DNA.

They live lives that have nothing to do with us, with me, monster in red and fur, nor you, reader.

How close do you think you can get to me? Can you creep in deerskin boots to where I lay? Am I smaller close up or far away? How is it that I always picture Grendel as a baby when he was slaughtered, and not a full-grown beast, six legs wriggling?

- Nadia Arioli

After Bruegel

Yet all men kill the things they love
- Oscar Wilde

Daedalus strapped wax wings onto his precious boy.
He was no dummy. He knew
what could happen. He knew
the recklessness of youth,
birds who leave the nest too soon.

But desperate to escape his own follies,
he built a contraption
to imitate the birds,
strapped it on his son,
then told him not to soar.

You know the rest, the bold escape,
the rebellious youth,
the fall, the splash.
The oblivious farmers tilling
their field, the fancy
that mortals could fly
lost on them.

Practical yeomen,
theirs a world of seasons,
doing all they can
to defeat the birds, their raucous cries
seeming to mock the men
who run at them, arms windmilling
like the wingless arms of the boy falling
into the sea behind them.

The birds try to tell the men, to help
their hapless brother falling,
but no one has time to listens:
the yeomen,

the fisherman,
the shepherd with his dog
not even the sheep will lift their heads

to heeds the birds crying
as they wheel away, flying
as close to the sun
as they dare.

- Dotty Le Mieux

Sometimes she ran on auto pilot, not particularly aware of what she was doing. Maria's feet led her through the door before she could redirect. Old memories. Instant hesitation. She didn't love being there. The place now seemed haunted. Her pupils widened in the low light. Scanning, feeling scanned, in a moment of mercy, she spied a friendly face at the end of the bar.

"Hi Joe. Long time."

Joe nodded in recognition. "Maria. How are things?"

"You know…another day. Been a few months, right? How you doing?"

"Buried my dog yesterday."

Maria faltered. "Christ, I'm sorry Joe. That cute little Spitz you had?"

Joe drank. Nodded.

"What happened?"

"Something got at her. Coyote most likely. I seen a bunch of 'em around. She come limping up to me half dead. Nothing to do for her. I had to put her down right there."

Maria pushed the swelling down her throat. She didn't respond.

The bar was a respite from the sunlight. Glancing to its front, she saw the dusk just beginning to color its pitted windows. Just then the bartender found her. Maria didn't recognize the young brunette behind the counter. She wore jeans and a t-shirt tied at the navel.

"Two shots please. Vodka. And a beer."

Maria had a history with the place. It was long ago, back when the jukebox was current. You could get fried chicken sandwiches on Saturday nights. The miners kept it busy. Now the business was just hanging on, frequented by a younger generation who would soon become the old. Tattooed with the same frustrations, thinking their problems were somehow unique. There was a new flat screen on the wall. It was tuned to a reality show in which a couple of women seemed very invested.

When the drinks came back Maria raised a shot glass with Joe. "To finding peace."

They swallowed in unison.

Maria read Joe's grizzled face. Not much hope left in there. His curly black hair was unkempt and greased over his scalp. It didn't hide the red in his eyes. She sighed, crossing one leg over the other. "So my kid wants to head to college next year. Wants to be a lawyer."

"You must be proud."

"I got no money for school, Joe."

"Ah hell, she can get loans. You know it'd be good for her. There ain't no future for kids here. Better she get out."

Maria threw back a gulp of lager. She figured right there that she and Joe would probably close the place. She looked around for the first time. To her right, down the back, the same dusty Phantoms jersey hung on the wall over the bathroom in the hall. There was just the one facility with a sign on the door that read "everyone." An older man had just finished up and walked past.

"She leaves and then I'm all alone Joe."

"We both know you ain't gonna stand in her way. She's strong just like you are Maria."

"You're right. I just don't feel prepared."

"Well, God knows we've all had a dose or two of that. But I sense you're better prepared than you know."

Silence crept in for a while. Then Joe broke it. "Maybe when the time comes you can do a fundraiser. I bet the fire station would help out."

"I suppose they might. Most of 'em knew Hale."

"Yep. And I suspect they'd want his daughter to have a future. Hale wanted that. You want that. Hell, if anyone deserves it…"

Maria called the bartender back. Another round.

She swallowed, staring into a void. "Deserves. That's a funny word, isn't it?"

"Well, like you said earlier…. just another day."

As new shots were poured Maria summoned the courage to look up above the bar and eye the framed photo collage of seven young children, each just out of focus. She examined their smiling faces. Their pearly teeth. The wooden cross that hung above them. Next to the collage was a photo of her husband and the sheriff. Shrines under store-bought frames. They hung there like shadows burned into the wall, traces of the past people were desperate to forget. Most tried. She and Joe couldn't. They were residents in a vault of ghosts.

Somewhere out there were places in which a future was still possible.

- Darryl Lauster

Millstone

April explodes on Carroll Street. *Sono a Dumbo*, a NorthFaced man in Timberlands shouts in his phone, misled by marketing. Magnolias, pink and white, amaze even celebrities I walk among, one dead tooth in my mouth, reckoning an implant's cost. Molar means *millstone* in Latin. *What did you bite down on?*, Costas Mastikatos, my dentist asked. I felt no crack, and somehow worse, no pain. I woke, spat blood, opened wide for the mirror – split simply in half, stuff in the gap, perhaps the seeds of raspberries I ate last night while watching Logan Roy die. His last act fishing a phone out of his jet's toilet. A Biblical millstone weighed hundreds of pounds. To wear one meant to drown. *It would be better if a millstone were hung around his neck and he were thrown into the sea*, Jesus said and smiled, I wonder with how many teeth.

- Hilary Sideris

Dreaming in Chicago: A Golden Shovel

after Gwendolyn Brooks' "Kitchenette Building"

The first days of summer are the dream
of long hours, envisioning a palette that makes
the eye water with possibility. Have you seen a
blank page as the first words of a poem giddy
their way across the screen? But the smug sound
of typing does not elevate this year of No, of Not
yet, of Go back and try again, of strong
No-thank-you. I lack plot, a violence like
the unraveling flood stuck in my throat. I rent
words from a thesaurus, feeding
my journal with lists of Chicago's pain, a
narrative alternative to what a good wife
should do: mix dreams with art, babies, and furniture, satisfying
the cravings tradition embeds in her body like a
coconut, cracked, milky, poured and dripping for a man.

- Jamie Wendt

I'm in the wrong place. A poetry reading. What was I thinking? Five years ago, I nearly failed American lit. I majored in physics and now work on the university maintenance crew. I mow, pick up dead limbs, paint lampposts, sow grass seed where needed, gather oak and sycamore leaves that cover the ground in the fall, and plow and shovel snow in the winter. And yet, I'm sitting in a lecture room on a sunny September afternoon, waiting to hear a poet read.

A warm breeze carries the smell of a smoking charcoal grill through the open window. Pigeons perched on the roof coo. In the distance the university band rehearses for the halftime show of the first home football game while the creative writing students sitting in the first row bob their heads to the beat of the base drum's boom, boom, boom. I'm in the back row near the door, ready for a quick escape.

I love fall. I need to get outside.

Oscar, my boss and friend, is in the wrong place, too. The hospital. Non Hodgkin lymphoma. I think it's from his exposure over the years to the herbicides sprayed on the university greens. It's just my hunch. I have hunches. He's getting chemotherapy, and, if all goes well, he'll be home in a few days. I'd be at the hospital with him instead of here except he isn't allowed visitors, a low white blood count thing.

Think positive.

My father, too, is in the wrong place. Prison. Or maybe it's the right place considering what he's done. Still. He's been moved from the over-populated, bad-news pen at Mansfield to a friendlier and closer correctional facility here in southern Ohio. Three more years, he says.

I fidget. I'm not good at sitting.

The poet isn't really a poet. She's a theoretical physicist. Maybe she's bipolar, a poet and a physics professor. She's been hired to teach in the physics department, which is the reason I'm here. I've graduated but curiosity and the love of science live on. A few physics students sit in a clump in front of me, hoping to be mistaken for future Einsteins or Curies—if not by intelligence, by coiffure—despite not having a clue about the workings of quantum field theory.

To be honest, does anyone truly understand quantum field theory? Quarks? Entanglement? Nonlocality? Things both particle and wave, both here and there? Get real.

Rocky, a physics professor who arrived the year after I graduated, introduces her, this poetry-reading theoretical physicist. I guess her age to be mid-twenties, only a couple years older than myself, but her list of accomplishments includes dozens of publications and a year-long stint searching for sterile neutrinos at the Stanford Underground Research Facility—also known as SURF—in South Dakota. She accomplished all of this while I mowed laps around the north green and the football stadium.

Would I trade places with her? I don't think so. Maybe.

Then, just as Dr. Sloane Kipkorir Kimani steps to the podium, I get a premonition, which is different from a hunch. A video plays in my head, a prediction of things to come. This happens and is sometimes accompanied by music. This time not. I see her sitting at my kitchen table, eating toast, drinking coffee—I assume it's coffee—as I can't see in the cup and premonitions are seldom accompanied by smells. Maybe Kenyans drink tea. This breakfast premonition is disturbing.

I've lived with the premonition gift—sometimes a curse—my entire life, and it still puzzles me. It makes me feel as if there might be something wrong in my head. My father says I'm disturbed, that I have mental issues. My brother thinks I'm possessed. My mother doesn't tolerate nonsense of any sort, real or imagined, and refuses to acknowledge these premonitions even when they come true.

A theory: My uncle Carl is color-blind, and this, he claims, gave him the ability to spot camouflage better than his army buddies who had normal color vision. Another uncle, Uncle Dave, went deaf working on the ground crew at Port Columbus, and yet he can sense thunder long before my aunt or cousins can hear it. "It's the vibrations," he told me. My premonition gift is a bit like Uncle Carl's color-blindness and Uncle Dave's deafness. You lose one sense, you become better at something else although I'm not sure what sense I've lost. My father, who was convicted years ago of a serious crime, says I've lost common sense.

Anyway, the reason the premonition is so disturbing has nothing to do with her being a woman or a Kenyan. Wangari Maathai was Kenyan, and she won the Nobel Peace Prize, which says a lot for Kenyan women.

"You can call me Dr. K.," she says, "although I have been called other things." She laughs. We laugh although I have no idea what other things she might have been called, whether they were good or bad.

I think we should call her Dr. Kimani. That's her name. We can say it. My last name is Clay. When I substituted at the local high school one spring—what a mistake that was—the students called me, "Mr. C." Really. Clay was too much for them.

She's pretty in a long and limber she-does-yoga sort of way, and she has a quick smile. She's smart. What's not to like? Nothing. Except I'm not comfortable with the idea of a woman I don't know eating breakfast at my kitchen table. Cass is the love of my life even if she is far away and our times together have become brief and unpredictable. What might she think if an attractive, smart woman is eating breakfast in my kitchen? Assumptions might be made even though absolutely nothing would, could, be going on.

Another thing: People make me nervous. I disappoint them. They expect more. My house is falling apart, falling down. Her sitting at my kitchen table—I only have two kitchen chairs and they don't match—implies a closeness I'm not comfortable with. My bathroom is so cramped you can't close the door when you sit on the toilet unless you do a side saddle sort of thing. The house leans to the west. The two upstairs bedrooms have sloped ceilings, and you don't dare stand up straight unless you are in the center of the room.

"Nothing," Dr. Kimani says, beginning her lecture. "Is there such a thing? If you take a volume of space, take out every atom, every particle, what's left?"

A creative writing student—they are easy to spot when dressed in goth—says, "Nothing."

Dr. Kimani smiles. "Yes, so it would seem. But there is something, something that causes that space to expand, to stretch, for the universe to get larger."

"But how...?" the poet asks.

"Maybe we need a poet to answer that question," she says, much to the joy of the poets and the chagrin of the science majors.

"Dark energy," one of the physics majors blurts out to regain status lost to the poets.

"Yes!" she says. "You're right. We call that mysterious thing present in a vacuum dark energy, and it's responsible for space expanding." She pauses, makes a face like she's confused. "We've named it, this something that exists where there seems to be nothing, but what is it exactly and why is it causing space to expand faster and faster? Is this energy constant or will it eventually decay and grow weaker, allowing the universe to contract? Poets are experts at making connections. Perhaps one can solve the riddle of there being something where there is nothing."

She pauses again, smiles, waits for a reaction. I nod. She nods back.

I think about this something where there is nothing. Oscar was losing weight and always tired. I told him to get checked out. He said nothing was wrong. Oscar is stubborn. Eventually, I drove him to the doctor, and she found something, the non-Hodgkin lymphoma, which is a big something. Another example: When my father was on trial, he swore he did nothing wrong, but the jury found him guilty, said he did.

Dr. Kimani begins reading Mary Oliver poems, which I like, and then she's back talking about the mysteries of the universe. "Dark matter, dark energy, what determines the speed of light? Is Schrodinger's cat dead or alive? The universe is expanding. How much can space stretch before it…" She makes a popping noise with her mouth.

I like the questions and nod again. She catches my nod and smiles.

She's wearing black slacks and a white blouse. I don't see any rings on her fingers although I have zero interest in any relationship. I'm just observing. Reporting what I see. Besides, a theoretical physicist would not be interested in a lawn-mowing, snow-shoveling guy who has premonitions and a falling down house.

I assume my breakfast premonition was flawed, a glitch, maybe the result of a neutrino, one of those ghost particles, passing through my brain.

She reads "As I Walked Out One Evening" by W.H. Auden, and I think about the mystery of time and my eagerness to get home.

The students, some of them, become restless, begin casting glances at the clock above the white board. It embarrasses me and is one of the reasons I chose not to teach, that and I don't like spending my day inside. The more they fidget, the more I smile and nod as Dr. Kimani talks. I'm trying to be supportive.

She finishes her talk and asks if there are any questions, which is a bad idea. There's always the awkward pause as the speaker waits for someone to raise a hand, hoping the question is not stupid, which questions can be despite what is often said about them.

"Yes?" she says to the guy with his hand held high—always a bad sign.

"Dr. P," he says.

"K," she says.

"Oh yeah. Dr. K. Do you believe there's intelligent life elsewhere in the universe?"

A stupid question. What does her opinion matter? This was not part of her lecture. It has nothing to do with poetry, or dark energy. What if she says yes? What if she says no? We need evidence.

"Well," she says, "we don't know. What do you think?"

No! Big mistake! This guy is going to give an answer that will keep us here for another ten minutes!

"My personal experience is that there are definitely alien beings," he says. He moves from his slouch to sitting up straight and then leaning forward. I'm guessing he's watched ET too many times, that he's a fan of Close Encounters of the Third Kind, Starman, and The X-Files. He mentions the Bermuda Triangle, UFOs, and the movie 2001.

"Interesting," she says, when he pauses for dramatic effect. "Any more questions?"

I pray there will be none and my prayers are answered. After Rocky thanks everyone for coming, I jump out of my seat and am pushing open the door when he calls my name. "Russ! Hold on a second."

I step back, think, Shit, what now?

Because it is dinner time and the smell of pizza is drifting from the cafeteria, the students do not linger. Rocky motions for me to come down front, and I think he's going to ask me to stop mowing outside his classroom in the mornings or if I could repaint the lines in the faculty parking lot, someone keeps crowding his space.

"Sloane," he says, "this is Russ." He turns to me. "I mentioned that you had a room you wanted to rent." He turns back to her and adds, "It's within walking distance of campus."

She holds out her hand, and we shake. She has long fingers and unlike most handshakes I encounter, her hand does not get lost in mine.

Okay, technically, I have a room for rent. Not so technically, two potential boarders have turned down the chance to rent that room. One guy, who worked summers in a turkey slaughterhouse in Iowa, groaned when he saw the room. “Thanks, I don’t think so,” he said. The other guy, a ROTC student who spends every other weekend crawling through mud and playing war games, got as far as the kitchen, and said, “Ah, no thanks.”

I bought the place when I heard the school was going to tear it down. Bought it for almost nothing except I can barely make those almost nothing payments in addition to my student loans. Renting out the spare bedroom would help a lot, but there is no way I can rent to a woman for reasons I’ve already mentioned. Too many assumptions.

Dr. Kimani would not be happy there.

I want to say I’ve already rented the room and save myself the hassle, but I say “Yes,” because Rocky and Sloane would see I was lying.

There’s an awkward moment. I’m not sure what comes next until she says, “Do you have time to show it to me? The room?”

I have tons of time, but I feel like I should warn her first about Yogi and the small bathroom and the house falling down and needing paint and that the windows rattle on windy days.

“Sure,” I say, glancing at her feet, thinking, if she’s wearing heels, she would not want to walk the two blocks, and we might postpone this awkwardness indefinitely. But she’s wearing running shoes, white ones that look new.

Minutes later we’re walking down Maple Street. She asks if the stories about the Halloween celebration on Court Street are true, when I graduated, if I enjoy working on the maintenance crew, do I walk to work. I do my best answering her questions while trying to find a way to warn her about the house. But then I think maybe it’s best I don’t say a word. The shock of seeing it will take care of any thoughts she has about renting the spare room.

“There,” I say when we round the corner. “That one, third on the right.”

I think she’s going to stop in her tracks, but she says, “Close to school. Convenient.” Maybe she’s looking at the wrong house.

“I have a dog,” I say as we go up the front steps. Yogi is only two but he’s a bear. “He’s huge.”

“I like dogs,” she says.

I open the door and Yogi charges. At the last second, he puts on the brakes, stops inches shy of Dr. Kimani, sniffs the air and presses his head against her leg.

"Oh, you are a pretty boy," she says.

Most guys step back when they first encounter Yogi, but she rubs his head with both hands. Yogi wags his tail. She's not paying attention, noticing all the warning signs.

"Want to see the room?" I ask.

"Sure," she says.

We climb the steps upstairs with her leading the way. Her butt swings back and forth in front of my face, and I stop halfway up to give her more space.

"On your right," I say. "My bedroom is on the left. Watch your head, the ceiling is low." She glances at my room—the bed is made, give me that—and then ducks into the spare, looks around, and peeks out the window, which is cracked but clean.

"The window rattles when it's windy," I say. "A small bed would fit, but there isn't much room for anything else."

"No," she says. "It looks perfect."

I look at the room and wonder what I'm missing. "Better see the bathroom," I say. "It's downstairs and it's small."

We go down the steps—no railing, no banister—one misstep and it's ass over tea kettle. I lead the way down a narrow hall off the kitchen. The tub has claw feet, and the shower is a makeshift hand-held hose with a nozzle. I've described the problems with the toilet. The mirror above the sink is old and the reflection is distorted. I hold the door so she can look inside.

"Okay," she says stepping back. "How much and can I have a shelf in the refrigerator?"

"I'm sorry," I say, convinced I haven't heard her correctly. This is no place for a theoretical physicist.

She repeats the question and before I can answer she says, "You didn't mention price. How much? Fifty sound fair?"

Fifty? Seriously? I'd been asking one fifty, but then no one had signed on at that price. Fifty a month would barely cover the extra cost of utilities.

"Fifty a week. Two hundred a month," she says, "and one refrigerator shelf is mine."

I've bungled the entire deal from the get-go. "But the bathroom. Isn't it too small for you? There's no lock on your bedroom door."

"Do I need one?" she asks.

"No, no," I say. I look to Yogi for help. "You sure?"

"You're not much of a salesman," she says. "Yes, I'm sure. I can walk to school. I won't need a car. This is perfect."

I look around the kitchen, try to see it in her eyes. I don't see anything remotely perfect.

"Okay," I say, thinking she won't last a month and wondering what I'm getting myself into. "It's a deal."

I feed Yogi while she's writing a check. I'm hungry, too. "I'm going to pop a frozen pizza in the oven," I say. "You're welcome to some if you like." I'm trying to be polite. I don't expect her to stay.

She hands me the check, two hundred dollars, a full month's rent. "Sounds good," she says. "If you don't mind."

So, I turn on the oven, get out a couple glasses and check if there's enough iced tea in the refrigerator. We sit at the wobbly table in the two unmatched chairs and talk about dark matter, dark energy, and the mystery of those ghost particles, neutrinos.

With the extra two hundred bucks a month, I can fix the rattling window and put a lock on the bedroom door for her peace of mind. A coat of paint, something bright, on the kitchen walls would cheer up the place, and a couple more chairs for the table would be good for when Oscar visits. I'll grow a sweet potato vine in the window. Real homey.

Just as my premonition predicted, she's going to be drinking coffee at my breakfast table. Coffee or tea and toast. Maybe yogurt sprinkled with granola. Months from now, people will talk, the other guys on the maintenance crew and maybe a few faculty members will give us the eye when we walk to campus. They'll look at me and grin like I'm keeping a secret. Some brave or nosey soul might even ask if there's something going on between us, between Sloane and me, and I'll tell them that there's nothing, absolutely nothing there.

- Roger Hart

What Belongs to the Moment

after Don Penn's photograph, The Butoh Dancer

Stirring stardust particles
from the starkness
of abandoned barn with its weary floorboards
and the swirling mist
of double exposure.

Body empty, deep and wide
thread of life pulls, unravels,
erupts, recedes. Rhythms inside
rhythms. From solar plexus
mountain trembles, shoulders comb
the clouds, river slows from eyes.
Spiders tucked inside palms,
smoke clings to thighs, arms
infinite branches to snag duende.
Feet transmute into the underside
of planets. Body an evaporating
cobweb, a long bag that sways
into the dance of darkness.

What silence can conjure.
What moment can beckon
from the void.

- Rikki Santer

Nearly Uncles

Up before dawn at the cabin on the Wapsipinicon,
Richard, Edward, and me spend the morning
in the duck blind shooting holes in the sky,
little blue and green wing teal folding with a snap
at a lucky shot, the mystical physics of flight
losing to the hard reality of kinetic energy
and the myth of gravity. Too young for coffee
I drink coffee from the dented steel Thermos cup,
steam curling into the rising fog, wet Lab
leaning into me for warmth and the bite
of cookie she knows is coming between sips.

In the bright light of a Bluebird day the teal
are ephemeral darting dragonflies.
More are missed than are hit, but Babe, like us, is OK
with only making the occasional retrieve. A Canadian wind
accompanies us in the blind. Cattail stalks wear rings
of ice that grow as the water quiets, reaching
for each other in an effort to close the bed
and breakfast, evict the disruptive birds,
ready it for the quiet and respectful winter creatures.
When the marsh freezes the ducks will leave,
and so will we, retire to sheltered woods and uplands,
carry our destructive passions elsewhere,
leave this place alone.

After supper the three of us, wrapped in a wreath
of Edward's Marlboro smoke, play cribbage
at the scuffed turquoise colored table. Too young for beer
I share a beer with Ed while Clamato and Vodka
whittle away at Richard's articulation. Hand gestures flap
wider and wilder like flaring waterfowl, speech regresses
to barking quacks and mumbled feeding chuckles
while the pegging count exceeds thirty-one
and the math of fifteen two fifteen four pair for six

becomes as incomprehensible as theoretical physics.
Play stops when Richard decides cigarette butts
are hors d'oeurves and Edward shuffles him off
to the bunk with the firm elbow grip of long practice.
Brothers to each other, nearly uncles to me,
I understand now this was one day in a long season
in which leaves had begun to fall,
ice had begun to form.

- Sean Whalen

At the Des Moines Ordnance Plant

– 20 January, 1944

She works the cartridge line, a golden island
surrounded by golden birds.
Shell casings twinkle and ring
as box after box dumps on the open table.
The 50 caliber are big around as a thumb,
able to take down enemy planes or cut a man in two.
She sifts the pile, the metal cool in her hands,
thumbing the sharp rim where the bullet seats.
The air squats like a penny on her tongue.
Her ears ache with the singing of the brass.

She runs her fingertips over each one, eyes closed,
imagining the shell sliding smoothly in the chamber,
the WUMP of ignition, the spent cartridge, her spent cartridge,
ejecting, spinning like a gyroscope, falling to the sand
or water or jungle mud, tastes the smoke,
hears the screams. She is a sister of war.
She knows wrecked bodies, blood in the food,
the moldy odor of rot. She caresses the casings
as if they were the damp brows of her brothers,
holds them like cold fingers, presses one,
then another to her lips.

- Sean Whalen

Sherd

On the gravel
bar a fragment
(figment)
of broken pot
washed from
the midden
tumbled
downriver
a pattern
from twisted
hair rope
vanishing
under the
scuff and rub
of shifting sand
undulating thumb
prints along
the rim
soften
(softens)
my thumb
brushes
the delicate
impressions
We touch

- Sean Whalen

Patterns of Leaving and Return

Women in abusive relationships return to their partners an average of seven times before they finally get free. For someone who's never experienced the terror and dependency of domestic violence it's hard to understand. Why would anyone go back? Why return to the abuse?

It's complicated. By love and lies. By shame and poverty.

By the stories we tell ourselves to survive.

Once upon a time, there lived a woodcutter and his wife. There's a famine in the land and the whole family is starving. The father and stepmother decide to sacrifice their children to save themselves, but the kids overhear their parents. Later that night, Hansel slips outside and fills his jacket pockets with small white stones.

The next day, as their parents led them into the dark forest to cut firewood, Hansel drops stone after stone, and leaves a trail that he and his sister can follow home. Their parents build a fire and leave them to sleep while they work. It's late when the children wake up and discover they've been abandoned. When the moon rises, the little white stones shine brightly, illuminating the path and they follow the trail home … returning to the parents who deliberately left them to die.

They make an impossible choice, still, where else would they go? Hansel and Gretel are only children, but some women make that same impossible choice every day.

Unfortunately the trails we lay down nearly always lead back home.

The first time John hit me, I'm out the front door in seconds, sliding behind the wheel of my silver Toyota Tercel, tears running down my face. I take the back streets from his cabin at the lake to Pipers Lagoon Municipal Park.

By the time I reach the parking lot, my tears have stopped. I haven't brought a coat, so I wrap my arms around my chest, scant protection from the cold April wind, as I walk down to the water.

John's my first serious relationship. I'd moved in with him after a couple of weeks, and we're already engaged. I'm eighteen. He's twenty years older than me, and a world apart from the boys I'd dated before him. I've left behind everything I know about relationships, and have no map to show me the way ahead. I only know I love him, and he loves me. I don't understand why he hit me.

I walk along the shingle, my feet sliding on the smooth stones, the sound of surf filling the spaces in my head. It was nothing, I tell myself. He didn't even hurt me. And that was true. It was the surprise of being smacked across the backside like a child that had left me in tears. It must've been a mistake, I tell myself. After an hour at the beach, I retrace my tracks back to my car, and follow the white lines at the edge of the road, back to the cabin, back to John.

He flings open the front door as my car pulls up. He's crying.

"Forgive me," he begs. "I'm sorry. I didn't mean that."

I allow him to pull me into his arms and I start to sob, relieved to discover it was a mistake after all. He holds me tight, and I soften into the shelter of his body. When I stop crying I tell him I forgive him. I love him. And I mean it.

Our wedding plans continue.

I have arrived in a dark wood, but I don't even realise I'm lost.

Their father was overjoyed when the kids find their way back home. He regretted leaving them in the forest. That's what he said, at least. The period of remorse and apologies is part of the abusive cycle. Their stepmother criticises them for taking so long, as if it were their own fault they'd been abandoned.

But it doesn't take long for hunger to creep in again. Their stepmother stares at the half loaf of bread left in the pantry and calculates what remains against the number of mouths to feed; she decides they must rid themselves of the children once and for all.

We've been married a few months the next time I run away. We're living in a second-floor apartment downtown Nanaimo, next to the Tally Ho Travelodge. When we first moved in, the walls and ceiling were brown with old cigarette smoke and splatters of thrown coffee that makes the living room look like a scene from an 80's slasher movie. It takes me days to clean and paint. I like feeling like I'm wiping the slate clean, erasing their past, and beginning again for us. It's our first home as a married couple.

I try to be the best wife I can. I cook, clean, dress in the clothes I know he likes, but John still loses his temper with me, though he's always torn up with remorse afterwards.

On this particular day, John has been yelling at me all afternoon. He didn't like the way I looked at one of the guys in our life drawing class. He accuses me of flirting. When I protest that I never even noticed Matt, he accuses me of lying. Reason, logic have no impact on his accusations. He tells me he's always watching me. He tells me he knows me better than I know myself.

"You're a slut," he says.

The air between us hums with tension, stickier than the old coffee I washed from the walls. I feel the violence coming. My body tenses, expecting the shove that will send me into a wall, or the blow I won't see coming. I'm doing the dishes, looking out the kitchen window, across the busy street to a small playground.

My hands are submerged in the soapy dish water when he steps out of the kitchen, leaving me momentarily alone and I'm out the front door, running across traffic, through the chain-link fence till I drop to the grass under the monkey bars.

I'm away from the claustrophobic tension of our apartment, but I still can't relax. I try not to look behind me, afraid to discover he's following. He's probably watching from the window. The thoughts in my head are so loud I can barely breathe. What is wrong with me? Why do I mess everything up? Our arguments make me lose track of who I am. I yank up fistfuls of grass and knock my head repeatedly against the iron upright of the monkey bars. I love him and he loves me. Why is marriage so hard? The streetlights above me flicker on, a line of white lights leading back home.

I sit still. Slowly the fragments of myself that fled from his anger return.

What am I waiting for?

I return to our apartment. Apologies tumble from his lips. He's crying. I'm crying.

Sometimes the trail is short, no further than the opposite side of the street. I'm walking blind in the forest, returning home because it never occurs to me I can do anything else.

The children overhear their parents' planning to abandon them in the forest a second time. When Hansel tries to go outside to collect more stones, he finds the door locked. He's too small to reach the key.

The next morning, their stepmother gives them each a single slice of bread for breakfast, Hansel crumbles his into breadcrumbs and leaves a trail as their parents lead them deeper and deeper into the forest. Hansel leaves a trail because even though they've been mistreated, all he can think about is getting back home. They don't have any place else to go. They can't imagine a different life. All they want is to return home.

We move again, this time to a single-wide trailer miles from the city. We only have one car now. John had an accident in his shortly after we married, so he's taken my car for his own. I spend long days isolated while John goes to work. The trailer is a dark place, set deep in the trees without neighbours close enough to hear his shouting, or my cries.

Sometimes when I'm alone, the sound of seagulls landing on the tin roof sends me into a panic. Their feet make a scraping sound that forces me out of my home, down the street, to the shore. I could leave that way, I tell myself. Pile my clothes on a driftwood log and swim out until I can't swim anymore. I've read that drowning is an easy way to die. It doesn't hurt. But despite the constant fantasy, I don't try.

When I do run, it's a Saturday afternoon in July. John hasn't stopped yelling at me since breakfast He tells me how useless I am. And I believe him. I mess up everything. He says I do it on purpose to frustrate him. I don't think I do. I don't mean to. I can't think anymore. The screen door slaps shut behind me. I'm cradling a broken rib as I hurry down the gravel road, away from the trailer, away from the beach, and towards town.

Twenty minutes later, I pass people washing their cars, mowing their lawns. My tears have dried and I keep walking. I promise myself that I'm not stopping. I'm not going back. He doesn't love me, not really. Why do I go back? The road gravel cuts my bare feet, the trail I leave is in drops of blood not breadcrumbs. Occasionally, I step onto the soft grass of a lawn, but I'm constantly forced to return to the road.

My steps slow. My feet hurt. I stop. I could approach a stranger, interrupt someone's Saturday afternoon to ask for help, but I don't have the words for that. I imagine how I must look, with streaks of mascara on my cheeks, and face blotchy from crying. I'm embarrassing. And who would I call? Where would I go? After eighteen months of marriage I have no friends of my own. And I can't bear the thought of calling my mom, seeing the "I told you so" on her face. She warned me against marrying John. But I loved him. I love him. I thought he would be my family. I thought he would keep me safe.

I sit at the side of the road, arms wrapped around my knees, head down, waiting. It's another ten minutes before I see John. He pulls up beside me, leans across the seat, and pushes open the passenger door. Neither of us says anything as I get in. He drives us back to the trailer. Inside he soaks my feet, tends to the cuts. Apologises. I look away.

This is not a new path. I don't know where it leads, but I know it doesn't lead back to the life I had before. That life, that girl, no longer exists. This home, this marriage is all I have now. There is nowhere else to go.

Hansel and Gretel sleep through the afternoon, their fire has gone out and it's dark when they wake up. They search for their breadcrumb trail, but the birds have eaten every crumb, and this time the children are truly lost.

They walk, searching for shining white stones, searching for any trail that might lead them home. They walk throughout the night and all through the next day until they're faint with hunger. They are hopelessly lost, but to stop would mean accepting their deaths, so they keep going.

We move to a new city, to a ground-floor apartment, in a big apartment block on a street filled with big apartment blocks. We've been married for almost three years; and I have run away and returned many times.

This night is bad. I'd been caught in a snowstorm, and was late home after picking up his son, plus I'd bought him the wrong brand of cigarettes.

Later, after the rage and the hurt, I pick myself up from the floor, cook supper, and when he steps into the bathroom to run his son's bath, I stuff bare feet into running shoes and slip out the French doors.

I run down the road in the rain, running between alternating pools of yellow streetlight and puddles of darkness. I cross the road, run down a side street to a big office building where I enter the empty parking garage underneath. Twenty minutes later an off-duty police officer finds me tucked into a corner, with my back to the wall. I have gone as far as I can.

"Can I help you?" he asks.

At first I don't know how to answer that question. This is the furthest my trail has ever led me, the first time I've ever been acknowledged when I am lost. Usually, my distress makes me invisible. I don't know what comes next.

The officer drives me to a community centre, and I call one of John's friends to come get me. I ask to sleep at their house for the night.

I do something different. I crack open our miserable little marriage, and let others see inside.

John picks me up later that night, and I find myself back home where he says I belong, but I have forged a longer trail out of the forest than ever before.

The children are exhausted when they stumble upon the gingerbread house in the middle of the dark woods. The house is built of cake, the windows are made of spun sugar. The old woman who lives there tricks the children. She locks Hansel in the stable to fatten him up and forces Gretel to work.

Gretel is clever. Eventually, she tricks the witch and traps her in the oven. Gretel frees Hansel from his cage, and they fill their pockets with jewels they've found in the gingerbread house. Then they look for the path out of the forest. Once again, they are heading home. The children could go anywhere. Instead, they go home.

The last time I run is on a chilly February morning. It's almost five a.m. and I have only just drifted off to sleep after a night spent fighting when John kicks me awake.

"Bitch," he hisses, pitching his voice low, careful not to wake his son who's sleeping in the other bed. "You can never leave me, understand that. You lying bitch–you promised, you swore, till death do us part, you're nothing but a worthless whore."

With a second kick to my back, he gets out of bed and goes to the bathroom for a smoke.

I'm wide awake. I know it's over. He's never going to change. And I have no time left to be careful. Quietly, I get up and slip on my jeans. In the living room, I pull my coat over my nightdress. My shoes are at the back door. I don't have time for socks. The patio door glides open silently. I step into the darkness and pull it shut behind me.

Once out of the apartment, I run. I have a few minutes before he realises I'm gone, then he will have to decide whether to wait for me to come home, or to wake up his young son and come looking for me. I'm counting on him waiting–I've never failed to come home before. But not this time, I promise myself.

My feet pound on the pavement as I run north, away from downtown. I turn off the main road, follow the alleyways and the side streets, eventually slowing to a walk. John drives this city, always keeping control of the car, while I walk and ride the bus. I know the hidden paths. I'm out in the city in the dark and I feel safer than in months.

I emerge onto the Esplanade and walk along the seawall. The night sky has lightened into silken grey when I chose a bench to sit down. Waves roll in over the wet sand. Seagulls cry out as they wheel overhead and began their daily search for food. I watch, reveling in their acrobatics, their freedom. I want what they have. It's not raining, just cold, and I pull my jacket tightly around me. I slow my breathing and focus on staying warm. I have no socks, no sweater or even underpants. But I have my coat, with my wallet and phone book pinned into the pocket. Each time I left, I'd learned something new.

I sit on the bench for an hour, until the Sunday morning joggers and early dog walkers come out, then I get up and walk to a bus stop. In Oak Bay I use the bank machine to withdraw half the money from our joint account. Then I board another bus heading downtown. As the bus goes past our apartment, I stare at the closed curtains, and wonder what is happening inside. Does he realise I'm gone for good this time?

I buy a Greyhound bus ticket to Nanaimo at the terminal. I have an hour to wait, so I buy socks from the drugstore and wander into Market Square. Now that the adrenalin of my escape has dissipated, my stomach rumbles. I look for food and end up in the bookstore instead.

I pick up the latest Grisham thriller to escape into on the bus then I wander around the store wasting time, ending up in the self-help section where I notice a book called Getting Free-End the Abuse. I look around to make sure no one is watching before I pick it up. I stand in the store and read the introduction, and I realise for the first time that I am a battered woman. I'd heard about halfway houses and women's support lines, but I didn't think any of that applied to me as John rarely punched me.

I sit the thriller on top and pay for both books.

I promise myself I'm getting free.

Aboard the bus, in the privacy of my own seat, I open the self-help book and begin to read. I need to try and understand.

I thought I could leave any time I wanted. For three years, I left all the time, running away when I couldn't cope with the anger and abuse anymore. I was the one who made the choice to go back. Since marrying John, I was estranged from my family, and cut off from my friends. I'd lost control of my car, lost any job where I earned enough money to financially support myself, and lost all sense of self worth. But it had never occurred to me that those things might impact the decision I kept making to return. Only when I was sitting on the bus, my escape finally in motion, did I understand that I had always made the choice to go back because it was the only choice I could see.

In the solitude of my bus seat, I finally saw the truth.

My sister picks me up at the bus station in Nanaimo. She drives me to my mom's house where I plan to tell them both about what's been happening. I still didn't know where I'm going, but for the first time I know not to follow the trail back.

In Hansel & Gretel, the children meet a duck that helps them cross the river and get back on the right path. Once again they are searching for the trail that will take them home. When the children get there they discover their stepmother is dead. Their father is overjoyed to see them. All their cares are over and the three of them live happily ever after.

But fairy tales are not the real world.

For three years I left and returned over and over again. I kept laying down trails, and always returned to the home that was my marriage. But the happily-ever-after was never waiting for me when I got there.

In the end I had to break the pattern. I had to leave that well worn path behind and break trail in a new direction.

To get free, I had to start a new story.

- Alison Colwell

False Dawn

You thought nothing could be worse than childhood 'til you found yourself at the end of the seemingly endless nose dive of your twenties, and so, still with that hubris of the younger self you've yet to outgrow, you enter the next decade clearing a path through the rubble, the debris from the crash, the destruction from those bombs you dropped — you couldn't fly straight (no one can), but then there was that button you kept accidentally bumping into — the angels and the ancestors and all of us other folks, who just happened to be around, we understood, you were distracted or drunk and the switch was red after all, you're human after all — it's something about the rods or maybe it's the cones, what it is, is that shade of peony and the unconscious desire to do the things you know damn well you're not supposed to; but would you look at that, you've found your shoes and a can of food and you've got yourself a pretty good map, you think, you're not sure exactly, it's really just another scheme and even though sometimes you can't read your own handwriting and most of the time you never follow through, you're pretty sure there's a way out of it all because of a little light shining through the soot; you're walking now, in that general direction, and, careful not to cut yourself on shrapnel for the first time in your life, you imagine the iced tea you're going to drink when you get back to civilization — or maybe it's a lemonade — nope, you're going to drink an iced tea and a lemonade, and when you start to think about how satisfied you're going to feel, like it will be the first time you've ever tasted something cold and sweet, you begin to wonder about the next thirty years — what could possibly be on the other side — and it's right then that you recall how your pop croaked when he was sixty and this kills whatever romantic yearnings you feel towards the crunch of ice and when the memory of the fear in his eyes — fear that grew as he neared his expiration — nags and nags and nags at your attention, this interrupts your fantasies of free refills long enough for you to stop and start to survey the damage, you know, just really take it in; and it's at this moment you begin a dramatic and panoramic three-sixty (because you still think life is a movie you get to star in) that's interrupted by the sour feeling in your stomach you can't name, and it's because the angels have crossed their arms and your ancestors are shaking their heads and as for all of us — all the other folks who just happen to be around — well, we already offered our condolences so now we're watching you soak in the gravity of this situation while we consider how glad we are everyone's starting to feel a bit more relieved; it's not the damage (as embarrassing as it is) nor is it the hell that awaits you (I'm using this term loosely here, of course, who knows if you'll meet the flames; maybe you'll be lucky and get to experience human hell — a few centuries as a few insects is a bit more likely; and no, in case you're wondering, there's no lemonade in human hell — there's no concept of a free refill either), our concerns no longer have to do with the life you appear to have jack-knifed off the highway of a decent existence and onto the wrong side of the universe (that was a pretty good run you had going by the way, what a crying shame), no, what it is, is what it's always been: it's your hubris; it's your hubris and your foolish fixation on cold beverages or whatever else you think is finally going to make you happy; you can't understand any of this, of course, you're completely ignorant, but lucky for you there's an angel nearby flapping its wings and now the wind is hitting you just right and just like that you start to think of your dear dead pop and the sin of doubt he confessed the night before he passed, and even if it is just like you to not consider what any of that means, you still notice the light coming through the smoke, smoke that billows in every direction and you notice how in every direction there is a little light, and it's then you realize you've never seen the sun.

- Corinne Hawk

Off the Edge

If I can't rave, I can't rave, I can't rave.
Maybe I'm not permitted to speak.
I'm a fresco chip disintegrated to powder.
I'm the compensation of small hands
packing rich earth around the roots
and the taste of licorice from the basil
off the edge of my lips. Past noon,
maybe later, I sit at a picnic table
beneath a roof on top iron poles
across from Kelly's Clams, and a seagull
is eyeing a fried clam halfway to my mouth.
The gull's claws are huge, a sickly orange.
I flick my plastic fork and feed this one
of Christ's scavengers, of Nostradamus'
and Allah's too, one on the boat of Immortals
hungry past beliefs and superstitious notions.
The bird gobbles the paunch of the clam
as if it's a gift from the dead. Some man
named G A R Y has carved his name in caps
across the picnic table green with brine.
I drink to this spear thrower, his unsteady hand.

-Richard Lyons

The Bereaved and the Unbereaved

An egret cleans an alligator so still it's purely part
of the mud and weeds. Murderers wear crimes
like wardrobe. I travel beside the rabbit and vole.
Beauty pays for love's shames. I'd like to become
a leopard on the periphery, devouring a calf
to keep its strength up. If I concentrate, I blend in
with the coarse boulders, light barely coming through
understory where rodents reproduce in the hundreds,
vulnerable heads folded over, terror and patience to grow.
At the cost of other forms of gestation, we humans insist.
The birds sing generous timbre and pitch varying so astutely
our brains barely tune our benumbed senses. David is bent
over his boxes, talking to his bees. They seldom sting.
They know love will strafe their wings. I rub his otter's belly.
The animal seems to accept the gesture and then nips my hand.
This agility takes a lifetime to master. Getting better at everything,
disciplines deliquesce, driving off pleasure and pain. A warbler's
nest blows from an oak and floats so lightly down. The fledglings
seem separated from their cry by wind. Are they the bereaved
or the unbereaved? Sometimes I jump off a roof, roll on the moss,
and squeak a peep-frogs' nuptial. I write colors. I dance with the dead.

- Richard Lyons

Opal with Blue Spots

The butterfly is a flame. Tourists have braved cliffs
to graffiti their names in the fleshy lobes of cacti.
I time travel to raze the library at Alexandria.
My soul is a particulate, a sketchy dissemination
assisted by kindness and generosity,
no ownership but what we pretend, my body
a phenomenon splitting the past and the future
like a river, like two hands severing dough
to make separate loaves. The mint sends runners
in all directions, fragrant leaves I pick from my teeth.
I lift a finger and tip the sun aside, my fingernail
illuminated bruise-blue in yellow outline. I blink,
lifting elephant ears to discover eggplants like newborns
besmirched with dirt and insect. I can't tell the elderflower
from the hogweed, one a poison, one an intoxicant.
I want to drink water with a sigh of algae and arrowroot.
Like soot, fungus spoors ride the air. I hear a dozen pigs
trundle a wooden chute. The hay for the miniature horses
makes me sneeze, my eyes watering like old cucumbers.
I coo to the geese, and they hiss. My falsetto, it seems,
is unconvincing. My raving doesn't really communicate either.
Genghis Khan fell from his horse. I threw the luckiest stone
I ever threw. It's an opal with blue spots
rounding at the bottom of a fast river. The water curves
shades of green the fish whisk with fins. They remember
to spawn and die. May we cease to embellish, our nerves die?
That's the ticket to the infinite, a drop of rain joining the sea.

- Richard Lyons

A Shock of Recognition

Once I saw a fisherman
who had caught a turtle instead of a fish,
a giant snapping turtle he laid on its craggy back
and stabbed through the neck with a hand-carved wooden spear,
leaving it half-alive but helpless.
It couldn't turn over, couldn't walk away,
couldn't even bite anything anymore,
only writhe and hiss and tread the air in mute agony,
and I whispered to myself as I passed
my twin, my brother.

- Kurt Luchs

Great White Shark

Not entirely white,
she surges from beneath, camouflaged grey.
With a primordial surge she scoops the seal,
whole, into her cavernous cartilage craw.
Beyond the breakers, her three-inch serrated teeth
crush a live sea turtle's thick shell.
Small black eyes assess you.
You, center of the world, are an after-thought.
You are swindled on her way to better prey.
She is the hollow in you. The bottomless.
Seeking death, eating blood, she is
innocent.

- Elizabeth Hill

The Hamptons

Summer Friday at noon,
Leave your wretched job, the constricting deadlines, the frenemies behind.
Burst from the skyscraper's revolving door like a bullet.
Clamor into your friend's magic Toyota.
Surge down the LIE toward the Summer House.
Hear the wheels' solid purr beneath you.
Feel the rushed brush of the wind under your reaching hand.
Let it just touch the short, hard scrabble pines.
Zip up the yellow and white lines.
Marvel at the sparkle of the road.
Turn up the joyous Springsteen:
I wanna die with you, Wendy, on the street tonight in an everlasting kiss!
Sing loud as you flourish past the hapless hoard of cars.
Let the green and white signs flow by, lesser destinations for lesser people.

- Elizabeth Hill

Gaby, yes, Gaby, I've lost my train of thought. How did it come to wrack and ruin? Two days before Christmas we ran into Tricia. We'd been doing some last-minute shopping—or rather, strictly speaking, Gaby was shopping, and I was trying to manage the kids—and as we started home from the mall at dusk it was evident one of our tires had gone flat. We turned around and pulled into Sears automotive, where Gaby could get a discount, and they discovered we'd picked up a nail in the sidewall.

I saw Tricia sitting there as we filed into the waiting room. But the children had had too much sugar and were unhappy about being there in a way that somehow indicted me, and Gaby had been, not cross perhaps, but exceptionally businesslike all afternoon, which always seemed to cut me out. I was not in the mood for Tricia, or for anyone else, and tried to pretend I didn't see her. If I'd been alone, I would have snuck out and waited outside; I hoped instead that the years had made me invisible.

No such luck. After a few minutes I heard her exclaim and saw her put down the newspaper she was reading and wave. I returned the wave, awkwardly, and she stood and came over to where Gaby and I, no seats open, leaned silently together against a bare wall. She gave me a perfunctory hug, and I introduced her to Gaby.

"The last time I saw you," she said. "You were working at that grungy hotel restaurant I stumbled into one night."

"Yes, yes, I remember that," I said, disingenuously fumbling for the memory. "You were there with some guy, weren't you?"

"He is now the boss there," Gaby said.

"Oh are you? I'm sure then that it's much improved."

"No, not much," I confessed. "So what are you up to these days?"

"Well, I married, too, and my husband and I have a two-year-old. Charlie. He's such a delight. I've always wanted a child."

"Congratulations," Gaby and I said together.

"Those can't be your children, can they?" she asked, nodding at Celeste and Diego, who were locked in some kind of physical struggle. Celeste was now on the cusp of puberty, uneasy in her own skin, her body set to run away with her, and Diego, well, he was Diego, nearly eight, an exasperating little force, insistent now as always on having his way.

"No," I answered, looking back at Tricia. "They're up for grabs. We trade in children, actually, practically giving them away. Are you interested?"

Tricia laughed. Gaby, predictably, did not.

"You're going to break it," Diego yelled.

"Just give it to me," Celeste responded. "It's mine."

Gaby excused herself and crossed the room to break up the fight, which turned out to be over Celeste's Walkman. Diego was getting one for Christmas, and it couldn't come soon enough.

"Don't have a second one," I advised Tricia, hoping for another easy (and pretty) laugh. Hoping, too, to get it out before Gaby, who was already returning, could hear. "No matter how well the first came out." I don't think I delivered it well, under pressure, and I didn't get the laugh I wanted. Gaby, looking hot and frustrated, probably didn't quite catch it, but she wiped a lock of hair out of her eyes and gave me a dirty look that revealed she did catch that I was being secretive with Tricia.

"I just told them to take turns," she said, easing herself back into our conversation. "It's not so difficult." She'd also, I observed, sent them to separate corners. "Tricia," she continued, "what do you do?"

"I stay home with Charlie now, of course. I worked for the city before."

"And your husband?" I ventured.

"Dan's a defense attorney. Dan Gorman. You may have heard of him."

Yes, I had. He liked publicity and looked like a weatherman—and this was 1980, so just imagine the feathery goodness of his brown hair as we sloughed off Jimmy Carter and put Ronald Reagan on. Tricia had done well for herself, and I felt a bit crestfallen.

"Stop looking at me," Celeste called from her corner.

"It's my turn," Diego yelled back.

"No it's not."

"It's been three minutes."

"It's my fucking Walkman."

"Celeste," Gaby shouted, in two hard syllables, rather than her usual, mellifluous, Mexican three. They carried with them her condemnation not only of Celeste but also of the English language, and especially of me, who had sometimes advocated for it in this respect.

“Was she your girlfriend?” Gaby asked, when we were home alone, our brand new tire safely installed.

“No. Not at all. Why do you ask?”

“She’s a bitch.”

That was a big day in the Jarvis family for language; I’m not sure I knew before that Gaby knew the word.

“Why do you say that?” I asked.

“It doesn’t matter,” she answered, with a shrug. I didn’t know what she meant, but it had been a long day, and I decided it wasn’t worth pursuing.

Christmas was dreary. Why bury a holiday in a hole at the bottom of the year? The children woke us at dawn, and together we clawed through the heavy curtain of the day. Trying to smile, not complain, I did gift assembly with the disquiet of insufficient sleep and compensatory caffeine throbbing in my veins. Even the children just bided their time, struggling sporadically with their new Rubik’s cubes, listless.

After we finally got them tucked into bed—Diego still wore pajamas with feet in the winter—I poured myself a drink and took up my position beside Gaby on the couch. The wind had been howling in the chimney, nipping around the corners of the house, all day, forcing cold air in beneath the molding and through the French doors. We’d built a fire against it, and I was wearing the new sweater Gaby had given me. It was a bit too warm, in truth, and scratchy, but I left it on anyway, and despite it felt the alcohol begin to loosen my muscles—the first time I’d felt well all day. I turned to look at Gaby, who was lost in her own world. How long had it been since she’d made eye contact with me—or was it me who avoided it? Ah, what I’d read there once, hanging in the air between us. If it had been understanding, I thought, would we have arrived where we were then, and if not, then what had it been?

“I want a divorce,” she announced, still looking away, and the words skimmed over a pool of meaning. She no longer wanted my singing in the shower, my t-shirts balled up in our chest of drawers, my help with the dishes. She rejected my best attempts at humor, the prattle when I drank, the warmth I brought to our bed. Not a lot, I knew…I knew… and now suddenly nothing.

I saw myself stand, stride, grab the top of the Christmas tree, and swing the whole laden, sparkling thing through the air—water from the base tracing a broad arc across the room while Gaby screamed—and out through the living room window. All done by a certain me that I am not. I also saw a second not-me, this one lacking the strength for such a maneuver. If I had intended to do such a thing, I saw the ridiculous, staggering struggle it would more likely have produced. I remained seated and took my head in my hands.

"Is there someone else?" I asked when my blood had thawed sufficiently to speak. It sounded like a movie cliché.

"Of course not," she said. "Nothing like that."

"Then why?"

"Why? Because you don't love me anymore, and I don't love you."

And I don't love you. "But why is that? I know there's still something between us."

"But something is not the same as enough. You will stick with it, no matter how unhappy you are?"

"Yes," I raised my eyes hopefully. "I will."

"But," she said with some amazement, "don't you see that's the problem? Why would I want that?"

I dropped my head again.

"Then it's hard," she continued, "for the rest of us to be happy too."

It was not, I saw in epiphany, going to be up to me.

I wanted to say…but realized words wouldn't help. I wanted to pour another drink but knew how that would look. Was it worse because there was no one else, the rejection cleaner, not circumstantial or comparative, more fundamental, final?

She laid a dry hand on mine. "You are always so far away."

"I'm always right here."

"No you're not. I feel like I am always alone with the kids. And sometimes when I'm not I wish I was."

"I feel like I am always here, here or at work, here when I'm needed."

"And when you are wanted? You missed it when Celeste first walked. I called you to come, but you said it was impossible."

"I was here! I remember every detail."

Was my mother here too? I remembered saying I remembered it well, but memory is a ghost through which we worry our lives backwards. It walks through walls, scratches in the attic, leaves open cupboard drawers, and then there suddenly it sits, lifelike at the dinner table.

"When you are here, it's like you are holding your breath," she said.

"I remember Celeste walking. Not Diego, but Celeste."

"Taking no joy in anything."

"I remember Celeste walking."

"Don't you have anything else to say?"

I turned my pockets inside out and found that I did not.

Gaby had no plans to move out, so I made them quickly and executed them the following Saturday while she took the children to a matinee. They saw *Airplane* while I collected those things that were mine. Not many, as it turned out; I did not have things I cared about, which seemed part of the tragedy. To them I added things no one else wanted from my home and my mother's. Pots and pans lost in the backs of cupboards, an old mattress, a hard, rickety wooden chair. I moved them into an apartment stinking of fresh paint and of something worse than the paint, imperfectly masked. The only thing I took to which I had no specific claim was a refrigerator picture in crayon, which Celeste had made years before, of the family standing in front of the house. She and I were the largest, closest figures, both with red stick fingers, blue stick arms, and broad, green, semi-circular smiles.

In a new bathroom mirror I found a sadness around my dry eyes that seemed familiar. I didn't know how far up I'd flown until gravity brought me spiraling down. I can feel it still if I put my hand near my heart—my family ripped away, my marriage bleeding out.

When I had announced my intention to marry Gabi, my mother said, "She's just using you to get across the border."

Quite a commentary on a mother's love, I thought then, but now… had she been right? Was that all it was, whatever it might have meant to me? Maybe, but if so then Gaby changed her mind. She soon retreated, with the kids in tow, across the line.

- Sam Brunk

Build

I want to build a road to the moon. Not a straight, narrow roadway, with boring plain concrete and a yellow stripe in the middle, but a wide winding way, large enough for all the peoples in the world who've ever dreamt of going to the moon to walk abreast and never fall.

My road is going to be splendid. It shall be yellow and orange and black and purple with pumpkins lining the sides and midnight cats to guide the way. The bats will be free to hang from lampposts whose branches twirl like ballerinas. Phantoms will walk amongst you here, ghosts of your friends and your loved ones, and sometimes people you've wronged or that have wronged you. Sometimes it is love that they seek, sometimes forgiveness or an apology, but always company.

As they pass over the cracks in the road, dandelions sprout from the bones that the skeleton marching band dropped on their way to perform at the Headless King's Fortress.

His is not the only festival on the road, though. Along the way are Fairy Circles, as the Fae dance with the fates and tempt death himself, who, I assure you, can be quite the player.

The witches — you can tell they are witches because they do indeed wear pointy hats — will no doubt be carrying their cauldrons to the moon, to be closer to its power, and the boiling point of water is lower there so their potions brew faster. The witches are clever, but the occasional one will stumble across the odd pack of werewolves or a colony of vampires and will have to back away slowly. Some vampires will find you threatening regardless, and hiss at you. If this happens, do not worry, their mothers are usually not far behind, ready to wallop them on the head.

My road will glide through the clouds and far into the stars. It stretches far beyond where the eye can see.

Should you desire to find it, simply walk towards the moon, with a hop in your step, and a charm in your pocket and say, "Dear Moon, may I have this dance?" She will extend the road to you and when you arrive, she will be standing there, radiant in her gown of stardust, and graceful as the creatures she commands. She will stretch out her hand to you and smile.

- Eva Nemirovsky

Ephemeral

Against the graffitied wall of a bar bathroom, I kissed you. I held your face between my hands; you wrapped your hands around my waist, tangling your fingers in my shirt. We exchanged words of love and lust between kisses, forgetting to breathe in the process. That's okay though. Breathing doesn't matter when your lips move against mine, our teeth clash, our noses collide.

Someone flung themselves into the bathroom, leaping for the stall. We stumbled out of there, laughing, out behind the bar before we collapsed in a fit of giggles. You slurred your words, but I got the gist: let's tie our shoes together, throw them up over the lamppost — a promise of forever. Or, at least, until the cops came to take them down.

That's how we loved, back then: whispered promises in dirty bathrooms and temporary vows strung along electrical lines, behind the backs of pigs. In secret. I used to stare up at the moon and stars and wish that others could feel the weight of the promises we made. But whenever a shooting star passed by, all I wished for was a few more seconds with you.

I may not be able to promise you forever. I may not be able to promise you my future. But I can promise you now, and baby, now feels like forever.

- Eva Nemirovsky

Drapes

Your hands are small in mine, yet they have a strong grip that surprises me. They're coarse and the fingertips feel like strawberries because of all the raised scars from safety pins that missed their mark.

I see you dancing around the room when you think nobody's watching, draping one piece of fabric over another to create an effervescent gown of layers of lace that takes my breath away, and I wish you would wear it, but instead I have to watch you give it to someone else, who only tears and rips it apart.

So, when you come home at night, you climb into bed and cry because of all the things you've had to give up and all I can do is hold you as tears trail rivers down your cheeks and make waterfalls that land on my chest where they gather in pools on my heart. You squeeze your eyes shut to prevent this from happening, but I wish to god you wouldn't because your eyes twinkle brighter than all the dresses you've made for stars that will never last. You despair because you don't understand how it could get better, but I know that one day all the scars and tears will be worth it, because one day you will accomplish what no one else has, and your eyes will be wide open, rather than squeezed shut.

- Eva Nemirovsky

Quick

It was the summer before I went into first grade, and there was a pedophile at the house next door. I had a friend who was almost without a doubt his victim. I know this now because the things that went on that July and August among the neighborhood children, things that for a time electrified our days with secrecy, were traceable back to Julia.

Such a breathtaking little girl, only eight years old, with a face like a character out of Jane Austen. Full lips and a rosy blush to her cheek. Pretty tendrils escaping from her hair caught back in a bun. But Julia was odd. The first time I heard the word "asshole," it was from her mouth, with attitude. You'd have thought she was twenty.

She told unusual and obvious lies. Once she said that if you cut a black person he would not bleed red, and she nodded her head with absolute certainty. It was like she had seen it, and could not be dissuaded.

She gravitated toward anything clandestine. All of us loved pretending, and dressing up in hats and heels and pieces of adult clothing, but Julia thought of thrilling little scenarios for us to enact. I was too innocent to know these were sex games.

"Doctor's office" was a traditional favorite, alternating with "bride and groom" and "putting baby to sleep." She wore a castoff man's white dress shirt, called it her "medical coat." When I was her patient I would lie down on the divan in the den of her house in order to be examined. The tan leather surface slid cool as pond water under my hands. A window air conditioner rumbled and hummed and blew in the background.

For her doctor voice, Julia affected an ominous authoritarian tone. "I'm afraid we're going to have to see what the problem is," she'd say. "Pull up your shirt, I want to put this stethoscope on you and listen."

I complied. She used the metal lid of an old mayonnaise jar, put it here and there on my chest and stomach. She made circles on my skin as she pressed, then leaned down with her ear. She would stay that way for a while, thinking.

"Pull your pants down a little more," she'd eventually say. "I want to listen to your belly down low, and feel if you have any lumps."

I shimmied my britches to my hips and waited in excitement for the jar lid to touch me, and then she would slowly press inside the band of my pants, her fingers many inches below my navel.

I was aware that we were doing something dangerous, because the game gave me a throbbing anticipation between my legs. The feeling was like a rope that I wanted to pull on, it was leading somewhere. I was aware that if a thing should not be talked about, it likely should not be done.

Despite Julia's urging, I would never take my pants down past my hips. "Quick," she'd say, when the adults, playing cards and smoking in the kitchen, came our way. She would help me pull my clothes back up to my waist.

Other games involved boys and were played outside in the patches of trees that stood behind our houses. Julia gave Kenneth and Brian long weeds with tassels on the end. "Hold it right here," she said, and indicated her crotch.

"And pretend something is coming out."

"You mean pee?"

She thought a moment. "Yes."

So it evolved that the boys would run after the girls and try to "pee" on us. Julia herself had no modesty; she would squat in the woods rather than run to one of our nearby houses to use the bathroom. Not caring if we saw, she grabbed a big leaf or a discarded potato chip bag in the absence of toilet paper.

Julia had a younger sister, Joy, and a sweet mother. Beautiful too, and her daughters looked just like her. But their father didn't match with them. He parted his hair in the middle and wore round black glasses like someone's great-grandfather from 1910. He had thick red lips like a candy mouth, and was employed in some capacity at the big Baptist Church in town. He had a certain local fame as a musician and was known for playing the banjo. He liked to bring it out for visitors.

It sat on his lap, a big drum covered with tight skin. A long black fretted neck coming off of that. He strummed the strings with one hand and moved his fingers on the neck with the other. He played loud hearty tunes like Camptown Races, and slow mournful hymns like The Old Rugged Cross.

My parents seemed to like him just fine. Who wouldn't like a banjo player, offering coffee and live entertainment? Why then, did I feel such an aversion? "Listen to me," my inner voice said, and I heard it whisper to stay clear.

Julia and Joy's father was also a photographer. He had a film projector and our family had been invited to see home movies of their vacations to the Florida beaches or the Cherokee Village near Gatlinburg.

One night he came to our house and took pictures of me while I was sleeping. My mother showed me the best photograph, and seemed very pleased. He had moved in very close. My face and body were lit by the light from the hallway. The bed upon which I lay receded in shadow, so it seemed I was nearly floating. I looked angelic with my doll Heidi beside me and my fat little hands curled up on the pillow beside my head like I was holding a small surprise, or maybe a coin.

"I didn't know he took my picture," I said to my mother. We were sitting at the kitchen table and I held the glossy color 8 x 10. I searched my mind to see if I could remember anything. It seemed I did, a little. A shape shifting at the foot of my bed. Something dark, breathing and somehow liquid.

Why had she allowed him to do it? I did not like the fact that he had been in my room without my knowledge. I looked at my mother with suspicion.

"He volunteered to do it—a portrait, as a gift. Usually cameras needed sunshine," she explained. "He knows how to take photos in low light, so you wouldn't wake up."

A few weeks later, I was playing outside with Joy, and I had an idea. We would play doctor. I took her into the bushes beside the front steps of my house. She was four. I asked her to take off her pants and her panties. She did it without hesitation, then leaned against the red brick and pulled up her knees. I examined her little slit. Hmmm. I stroked my chin with a physician's concern. It needed medicine. I turned around and gathered a handful of fresh green grass, and patted it on her. When I did that, I felt the pull of the invisible rope between my legs.

I had barely applied the grass remedy when my mother came down the front steps to see where we were. "Quick," I said, and tried to help Joy back into her panties, but I was not fast enough.

"What are you doing?!" My mother stared at us in shock. "Aahhhh!" She drew in a hard breath; it was like the sound of dynamite a millisecond before the boom.

"Joy, put your clothes on, and go home. I will talk to your mother later. And you!" She jerked me to my feet. "Get inside!" She yanked me out of the bushes by one arm and began to spank me furiously, all the while dragging me back into the house.

She took me to my bedroom, and pushed me in the middle of my chest. I sat down hard on the bed. It didn't really hurt, but she had never been angry and rough like this. She slammed the door behind her. I had never seen her chin so pointed, her eyebrows so drawn into a vee.

"What did you put on Joy? Did you put anything inside?"

"No," I wailed. "It was just grass!"

"Why were you doing that? Why?"

"I don't, I don't know." I threw myself backward and turned into my pillow, sobbing. And really, I didn't know, but eventually she got the story out of me about how I had learned to "play doctor."

It was a long afternoon of solitary confinement. My comforting room was now a miserable prison, and I stayed there, lolling in anguish as I waited for my father to get home. My dolls stared in heartless apathy. One by one I threw them against the wall.

Eventually my father came home from work and I heard my parents murmuring and arguing. When my bedroom door opened my father looked at me in sorrow. He had heard about my crime. I felt a stab of pain in my heart. I saw that he didn't want to do it, but he knew he was supposed to be the executioner. My mother stood behind him, her forehead furrowed and her arms folded across her chest.

Seeing the two of them, I dropped cowering to the floor.

"Cathy, what was going on?" My father seemed genuinely concerned.

"We were just playing!" I was weeping uncontrollably again, my face like a broken plate.

"You know you can't play like that, now, don't you?" He moved toward me, then unbuckled his belt and started to draw it off. "Don't you?" His voice got louder.

"Yes, I know. I know." My terror grew. I think I blanked out as he pulled me face down over his leg. He began to slap me with the belt. I was wearing shorts, and the leather laid red u-shaped welts on my thighs as I cried out. He spoke as he hit me: "You. Can. Never. Do. That. Again. Do you. Hear me?"

Though he was beating me, I somehow still felt loved. He felt he had to discipline me, was all.

I was so very sorry they felt I had been bad. I could see with a tiny piece of my mind that I had been. But also, I was so sorry I had been caught. If only I had gotten us a better hiding place, none of this would be happening.

I saw my baby sister Susan standing in the doorway watching. She seemed to observe with great curiosity. Such seriousness, not smiling at all. She had just learned to walk, and held on to the door frame while she studied the scene. "Don't let her see this," I prayed inside my head. "Take her away." I tried not to cry too hard; babies should not see upsetting things, I believed.

After my Big Punishment, there was an Investigation. My mother was on the phone the rest of the evening, and the sex games were discussed. Joy's mother had told her youngest daughter to "never let anyone do something like that to her again."

It was still taking me a moment to register: now who had done something horrible to Joy? Oh right, that was apparently me. One family in the neighborhood decided that they were not going to let their children play with me anymore. They told my mother I was a bad influence.

Not play with me? Who did they think they were, so high and mighty? I knew I was not a dirty girl. The whole neighborhood had been involved. Other girls with shirts up and pants down. The boys with their disgusting pee-sticks, Julia the ring leader. Every time I thought about it, my mouth came open in indignation. Oh, the injustice! They had labeled me as something I knew I was not.

I learned a lot about the world then, from the way this was handled. It was not fair that I should be ostracized. I had been taught the doctor game by Julia, and then I had played it with someone else. It hadn't even dawned on the adults to ask further up the chain. Who had taught Julia how to play such games? I thought I knew.

Several months later, she came to stay with our family for a week. My mother's friendship with her mother was enough to override the scandal, I suppose. I don't remember where the rest of her family went, but it was just her. While she was with us, she came down with the mumps. My mother fixed her a bed on the sofa and covered her with the quilt from my bed.

I brought her juice and set it on the table next to her. She lay defenseless, her eyes closed, her skin flushed. One side of her face was blown to a fullness, like she had a cheek full of water. I saw her differently then. She was not a ringleader. She was only some fragile vulnerable thing, like a little bird in a nest. Her body, though sick, would recover. It was her tender spirit, residing in that body, that was most open to illness and predation. Oh Julia. What could I do?

My mother, meanwhile, had decided that I should try to catch the mumps from her and "get it over with." I had already had chicken pox and measles. "I think maybe if you kiss her," Mother said. "Just kiss her goodnight on her cheek, get down in her face. You'll probably get infected that way."

She stood watching. "A quick kiss," she repeated, and gently pushed my shoulder. "Go ahead, get close to her."

Reluctantly I leaned down. The off-smell of sickness mixed with the sweetness of her sweat rose from her body. Julia did not open her eyes or seem to know I was there. I did not want to get sick. No. But I submitted to what was being asked of me. It was my mother telling me I had to. I pressed my mouth to my friend's cheek and felt her fever on my lips. I did it, and then drew back, resigned. I would be sick, or maybe, I would stay well.

- Catherine Vance

People and Places Left Behind

A Prose Poem on the Hard Part in Our Recalling

Last night I listened to music from my teen years, both old love ballads and classic Rock and Roll, over and over, and over again. Listening to the music, the misty lens of its lyrics and the floating melody of sounds, made me think of all the people and places we leave behind on our journey in life. I felt a particular sadness about that time in our life when high school comes to an end and new worlds open, different worlds for each of us. Everything is unknown, and we are all eager and a little brash, a little scared and clueless, and happy and sad, and all at the same time. Everyone is hopeful as these new worlds open and take us in, though anxiety now marks our play with friends, and nervous smiles our parting. We seemed lonely, as well as sad, as we play acted so much of our own coming of age all those many years ago.

Life would be better for some than for others, harder and much shorter for some than for others, our lives now becoming serious adventures as life began playing for keeps. Drifting apart on different roads, soon different cities, different friends, different lives, always looking forward and making our way, with work and life, not knowing how much we would miss, for the rest of our lives, all those people and places we loved in our youth. Our younger worlds lost with the years, we pass each other unrecognized now, old age the perfect disguise, though our memory of those people and places of our youth can remain for us as clear as a bell.

With memory, life can seem unbearable. Yet, without it, there may be no real purpose in living. And underneath it all, the old anxieties still linger. This time mostly about being forgotten, or something like it, like being loved, if only for how we threw a ball or how we wore our cap or by the girl we walked away from without a last kiss and embrace and without a whisper that she would be loved for a lifetime. There's that vague feeling we have that an opportunity may arise for a great-do-over sometime in our life, to return to those people and places of our youth to say the right thing or to somehow make things right. That feeling, of course, is only an illusion, another phantom in the shadows of our time. Once the sun sets, we wait only for another, different daybreak.

Still, we might turn back to those people and places we loved, through the memories and shadows, the smiles, and the tears, and hope just once for something more, for something buried deep in those fields of gold that has always been just at the edge of our heart, a remembering that might allow us to turn towards home again, if only to say goodbye, with a smile and a sigh. Perhaps, it lies in that part of our recalling, of how long ago we lost so much by not really knowing how to say goodbye to those people and places that we loved and of how easily we let it all slip away.

- Edward Ziegler

Eight of Cups

If you turn around, you'll see you left
before realizing you'd chosen to. Behind you
is the wall of crenelated cups you carefully built,
filled with the relinquished contents of your pockets--
lip balm, loose change, handkerchief.
The space with one cup removed was your exit
as well as your entrance. And, yes, that's you,
the old man with the stick, red jacket and shoes.
You can only go in one direction now, old friend.
The bright, ambitious sun is eclipsed; you're guided
by moonlight, reflected and reflective. Walk along
whatever river flows between the cliffs and crags;
each empties into that place of all returns, the meeting
of sky and sea--green-blue, blue-green--horizonless.

- Don Hogle

Pier Forty-Six

I was walking among the geese who pecked
at crumbs in the turf of the reclaimed pier.
Helicopters chafed the clouds above the Hudson,
shuttling between the jagged Jersey skyline
and Manhattan's upward thrust. The city
cast its reflection on the water, and I was filled
with sympathy for the carnival of the whole
human project.
§
In high school, my buddy Jay and I pitched a tent
in my backyard as far from the house as we could.
Smoking cigarettes we stole from my father,
we were poised on the edge of the world.
Cicadas chirped their siren song, and possibility
splayed itself before us. Whatever it might bring,
we would brave it together; that much we knew.
§
At the end of the pier, through fog on the horizon,
I glimpsed the tiny figurine of the Statue of Liberty,
her torch lit like the tips of my father's Marlboros,
which glowed for a moment each time we inhaled.

- Don Hogle

Tracking True North

You're stuck with the vulnerability, so you might as well do something with it.
Julia Cameron

Go to the page with a heart as open as the heart of god.
Elizabeth Strout

In 1995, a flyer arrived in my old-fashioned mailbox that perched on a post at the top of my mile-long one-lane potholed driveway. I was invited to join a workshop based on *The Artist's Way: A Spiritual Path to Higher Creativity,* written by Julia Cameron with Mark Bryan, published in 1992 by Tarcher-Putnam.

I was a little put off. Higher Creativity? Really? I initially felt the authors borrowed too freely from 12-Step programs, and journaling and creativity techniques from other authors I'd studied, including Ira Progoff, Tristine Rainier, Natalie Goldberg, and Gabrielle Lusser Rico.

But I knew and trusted the woman offering the workshop. A clinical social worker, Judith Alexander is a long-time resident of Port Townsend, Washington, my birthplace. We'd co-facilitated workshops for at-risk adolescents, and I respected her way of communicating.

Although I don't consider myself a "group" person, and didn't really have the money or time, I signed up for the thirteen-week course.

Every Wednesday, for two hours, eight of us, all in our thirties, met in a rented artist's loft overlooking the sparkling bay that encircles Port Townsend. We shared creative yearnings to paint or write or sculpt or make music.

The Artist's Way was soon to become a mostly word-of-mouth best seller, with hundreds of thousands of "practitioners" all over the world. Julia Cameron, subsequently listed as sole author, advises three pages of hand-written daily journal entries called morning pages, a weekly solitary adventure called an Artist Date, and other exercises and activities called "toys." "Creativity is joy," Mark Bryan says, "A contact with the life force."

Each week, with Judith's facilitation skills keeping us on track, we completed weekly homework to share with the group. Despite my initial misgivings, the method "took." I'd kept a daily journal since elementary school, but it's nice to renew "permission" to enjoy that start to each morning, a sort of warm up to the day. The concept of Artist Dates continues to remind me to indulge the pleasure to check into a thrift shop or gallery or museum or to create a little patch of garden, entirely on my own. From the first session, what Cameron calls the trajectory of my life began, at first slowly, to shift.

From childhood onward, I planned to be a writer. My mother had a degree in journalism and history from Northwestern. She took her six children along on assignments for Sunset and used us as subjects for articles in parenting magazines. She gave me my first journal when I was in fifth grade, encouraged me to write every day, and helped me enter writing contests and attend writer's conferences. She and my father, an artist, went over every project or paper I wrote as if I were an adult. My father would tear my writing to shreds, and my mother would follow up in her rounded handwriting, always offering words of encouragement. Even in junior high, I'd stay up all night making revisions. When I was in seventh grade, my parents gave me E.B. White's *Elements of Style,* and my father took me to literature classes at the University of Washington as he earned his M.A. in English. I read the assigned novels assigned by Thomas Hardy, Thomas Mann, and James Joyce, and then we'd discuss them during the hour-long ride to campus.

In college, I was lucky enough to study with superb writing teachers who encouraged and mentored me. In my twenties, another mentor, a poet, found me the ideal job teaching writing to gifted and talented kids in the public schools. I earned an M.A. in fiction writing, published some work, and was encouraged by top editors, with an agent interested in seeing a novel.

As many women do, I blew up my own life. Immediately out of graduate school, I briefly married a nine-years younger man and worked as a counselor to support his musical aspirations and a sprawling mini-farm. I blasted out of that by entering sixty days of inpatient alcohol rehab. Within two years, against all suggestions for my well-being, I was dating a man with a four-year old child. He and the child needed me. Heck, even his ex-wife needed me.

Soon, I was a mostly solitary stepparent, as my new husband worked on merchant vessels overseas. I worked gypsy-style, racing between community and four-year colleges up and down the I-5 corridor from Edmonds to Seattle to Federal Way, to arrive, barely in time, for my next class, and then turn around and do it all again. I vowed to offer my young stepdaughter a normal life, as if I had a clue what that was, and spent my evenings engaged in what my stepdaughter called "krecting papers."

Once I embarked on *The Artist's Way*, though, I started to change. One night, when I arrived home from the group, my husband looked at me as if noticing me for the first time. "Those pants aren't very flattering," he said. The next week, when I received a call from a group member, my husband raged. "You never told me there were men in the class!" he said.

The second chapter of *The Artist's Way* is entitled "Crazymakers." It's about "personalities that create storm centers. They are often charismatic, frequently charming, highly inventive, and powerfully persuasive." Cameron states that to fixer-upper types, such partners can be irresistible.

I skipped through that chapter. "None of those in my life," I reported to my fellow artists. When I was halfway through the course, my husband "accidentally" erased my life's writing from my hard drive. A novice and reluctant computer user at the time, I had no back up files. Determined to make the marriage work, I wrote myself a formal letter of resignation from my writing dreams. It was better to give up than to break my own heart. I'd be a superlative teacher and stepparent instead.

When Alice Munro was awarded the Nobel, she said, "I write to comfort and please myself." I wondered how she managed that. Her daughter Sheila's *Lives of Mothers and Daughters* documents her mother's emotional absences. Judith Thurman's biography of Colette, *Secrets of the Flesh*, describes the famed French writer's sequestering of her daughter with a nanny, visited rarely and always held at emotional arm's length.

My own mother's journal, filled with poems and notes for projects, ends "I always thought I'd do something with my life. Now I see I should devote myself to these beings I've brought into the world."

For graduation, each Artist Way group member was to compose a collage that symbolized our lives. "Don't think too much," Judith said. "Just tear images from magazines or photos and slap them together any which way." Mine was giant, elaborate, and three-dimensional. I didn't notice until the group pointed it out that images of my stepdaughter appeared everywhere, and my husband not at all.

Cameron describes finding one's True North. Once identified, Cameron says, there is no turning back. Our lives gently, slowly, and sometimes tumultuously lead us toward the truth about ourselves, the choices we've made, and the opportunities we've abandoned. By 1996, my marriage ended, and by 1997, my job. I ended up living in a tent on the edge of Hood Canal, the frame of my dream cottage rising skeletal in the thick evergreen forest.

Until then, I used my computer more or less as a word processor, a step away from typing. Now, alone in the forest, I started to explore the Internet. Besides searching for groups focused on native plants, a passion, I stumbled back into Artist's Way. An international group was beginning a new series to explore Cameron's book. By the end of thirteen weeks, I was communicating with scores of artists from every corner of the earth, hosting guests in my now-completed house, and proposed to by a man who never met me but was certain I was the one. I was deep in the embrace and, on occasion, the flames, of a cyber world for which I previously held only contempt.

When that cohort graduated, several members wanted to continue. One offered to set up an e-group community, and I volunteered to co-moderate. We called ourselves AWgrads, and soon, again, attracted hundreds of members from all over the world. Artists arrived, found what they wanted or did not want, occasionally left in a huff, or, as I did, left to work full time. Artistic pursuits included quilting, jewelry-making, writing, painting, opera, musical theatre, scriptwriting, poetry, songwriting, pottery, ceramics, teaching, interior design, sculpture, playwriting, and dance.

In 2000, with the skills I learned from fellow AWgrads, I was offered a position as executive editor for an Internet start-up. From the forests of the Pacific Northwest, I found myself in West Hollywood in a fund-raising gathering hosting Hillary Clinton during her first senate race, in New York with Random House editors, and in Boston for a mind-expanding experiment facilitated by brilliant young physicists soon to be eradicated when the Twin Towers fell as they started their annual meeting at Windows on the World.

My new job was to recruit writers and editors to produce educational documents. From days spent observing whales, American bald eagles, and Pileated woodpeckers from my cabin, I lived in the CEO's Los Angeles living room where twenty-somethings all shouted at once about color, design, buzz, and monetization. My start-up experience was just as everyone said, if I'd known anything then about what anyone said: we worked from nine in the morning to nine at night, often seven days a week. We co-created a beautiful website filled with what I learned to call not writing but "content."

Then came the crash. The chief investor took over as CEO and moved in his brother and brother's best friend. By then, the co-founder and now former CEO and I were engaged. We flew to the island of Rarotonga where a Māori elder, Te Tika Mataiapo, performed our wedding ceremony on the beach. We snorkeled, hiked, and rode mountain bikes all over the twenty-mile island, and took a day trip to Aitutaki. We listened to a cappella singing that combines Maori tradition with Christian hymns and made friends who planned and attended our wedding and invited us to gatherings high in the hills.

When we returned to Los Angeles, my job duties had also been reassigned. My new husband and I both suffered what was once called a nervous breakdown. Now it might be called post-traumatic stress, or just plain grief, the loss of our Internet dream. We couldn't sleep, suffered terrible nightmares, and took turns weeping and consoling each other. While bicycling around Santa Monica, a block from our rental, I was hit by a car and lost my four lower front teeth. Surgeries to replace them were agonizing and inadequate.

I suggested we return to my cabin in the Northwest forest, and we headed north. We combined our possessions into my tiny cabin and planted wildflowers and vegetables in the raw damp earth, the bald eagles nesting overhead. We exchanged the frenzy of the start-up for harbor seals, river otters, coyote, bear, bobcats, cougar, Roosevelt elk, and countless species of birds I nevertheless attempted to research and record. We tried to find new ways to earn our living in the remote rural area, became deeply involved in environmental advocacy for preserving and protecting heritage forests and shoreline, took in pregnant foster cats from the county animal shelter and tended them as they gave birth, then had them spayed and neutered and adopted to indoor homes. We provided home health care for elders.

And then, out of the blue, my husband received a call from a public relations firm for which he'd previously worked, offering him a position in Manhattan.

Once again, our lives shifted. We sub-let an Upper West Side apartment, and I was introduced to the joys of theater, film, galleries, and readings. I found a writing group, and at my first meeting, heard one person say how she never finished projects, and another, just selected as one of the top writers under thirty awards, describe how it plummeted him into depression and now he couldn't write. I was stunned to hear my own writerly self-abnegation from the mouths of these, to me, successful people. When my turn came, I spoke of how I'd set my own dreams aside. As the group broke up, an elegant woman approached to shake my hand. "Thanks for your talk," she said. Her face seemed familiar. I'd just seen her supersized on a poster in the window of a famous bookstore. "I'm Julia," she said.

Now, back in the Pacific Northwest, I live my own True North. Writing comforts and calms me. As artist dates, I continue to learn the names of plants or birds. My husband and I cleared brush along our long narrow driveway. As we gently trimmed back thickets of huckleberry, salal, ferns, wild blackberry, and willow, we uncovered huge broad stones my father and his art school buddies placed there when they dug in that road by hand.

Buddhist teacher Pema Chodron calls this samsara, those births and small deaths we endlessly repeat. When I face any challenge, rather than handle it the way I always have, Chodron teaches, first do nothing. "Bring the breath to this moment," she says. I shift the patterns of a lifetime, perhaps many lifetimes, to land in in my own skin. Thoughts settle like dust on a mirror. I listen to the sound and my judgement of that sound. Then, gently, as instructed, I blow away the dust.

- Kirie Pedersen

Like Elijah, In the Year of COVID

Living hidden in the cleft of the packed city,
window on the half-light shaft
and otherwise bricked under,

you've been pondering the code of the bluescreen
for some answer,
starting gun, key episode, magnetic north for a life
in which it will make a difference
to have been good
without ever having been close.

Do you remember my friend Pearl?
The one who put on makeup in the hospital,
while planked flat on her back,
from a turquoise bag always within her reach.
Second skin, though no one came to see
in the pentimento of floor seven, unit B,
at night, when passing flocks of off-duty nurses
twittered like company fleetingly in the hallway
until the great silence was wheeled in.

I have never held a sparrow against my skin,
but I can feel in this moment
precisely its vibration in my palm
nervous and pressing forward toward flight,
bewildered at its incapability,
outraged at capture.

Some of us are brave in loneliness,
in dying, or simply in solitude.
Some intolerant of crowding,
or a bit queer and chronically unsettled.
Some bristle against fate's prickles with our own.
My dear friend, today I wonder
whether you and I are simply patient,

ready to wait if necessary for ever
hoping God will turn around and see.

- Jennifer M. Phillips

After the urgent care visit, I decide to visit the Museum of Natural History. I need something to get my mind off the blood. There is a temporary exhibition called "Beyond Cavemen", which contains remnants of hominids and early nomadic man. I saw an ad for it on a bus weeks ago, but never found the time for it.

There is a crowd of children on a field trip in the lobby. Different teachers hold up signs with different colors. By the time I pay for my ticket, one of the groups is beginning a tour with a youngish docent who is chirpy and has a perfected stage voice. "Everyone, follow me, and hang a right up ahead!" she calls, walking backwards. I linger shortly behind the group, pretending to be aimless, as if I'm engrossed by the list of donors marked by tier along the hallway. Ahead, I hear the tour guide ask if anyone knows what anthropology means. The study of man, a child calls.

The exhibition has been divided sequentially by chronology and hominid, a fast forward through our evolution.

Homo habilis: The toolmaker. Homo erectus: The firemaster. Homo neanderthalensis: Lost cousins. The docent lectures beside a habilis skull, points out the elongated forehead. "It looks more like an ape, doesn't it?" I listen along towards the back, taking in the free tour.

This is my second miscarriage. The first one was years ago, when I was too young. I only felt relief when it happened then. It was not a good time for me to have a child.

It still is not a good time.

I gaze at the specimens on the wall. A rock with many grooves, a rudimentary sharp edge. I imagine this very rock in a hand like my own, although much tinier and hairier, striking it against another rock with all my might. I imagine that hand running a thumb along the edge. Sharp enough. As the BCE dates shrink in the display case, the tools become more refined and sharper.

"This is the first sign we see of human cultural behavior," the docent explains to the children. The sentence makes my breath catch in my throat.

The group moves on.

"Homo erectus is the hominid that learned how to create fire.

How would fire help humans?"

"Warmth!" a kid calls out. The docent nods, but she's waiting for something more.

"You can cook!" another shouts. The tour guide's eyes gleam.

"Cooking! Yes!" she exclaims, launching into a new lecture about how cooked meat helped our brains develop more intelligence, leading the crowd and me along.

The tour guide is explaining how anthropologists can tell from the burn patterns of bones and debris that it was a purposeful fire, instead of a wild burn. The kids ooh and ahh, and crowd around the display case. I'm curious to how the wood looks different myself, but see no way around the throng of children.

Behind the group, through a constructed cave mouth entrance, are tombs. The first burials. A shaman with his jewels, a juvenile wrapped in a blanket, a woman found beside the remains of flowers. I notice the docent skips this part of the exhibition, and instead leads the children to maps of human migration across the planet.

I suddenly feel a wave of exhaustion. The physician's assistant warned me that the pain medication might make me drowsy.

I leave the group behind now to the end of the exhibit on my own.

"Don't worry. You're doing great," the PA told me during the examination, which I thought was funny. Like there was a right way to have a miscarriage. Finally, something I'm good at.

She prescribed me something to speed up the bleeding and something to numb the cramps, and thankfully didn't once ask how I was feeling.

In the courtyard outside the exhibit, there is an empty bench. I fall down onto it. My bones are so heavy, how can I carry them around? My eyes droop. I let them, too drained to fight my body any longer. It will always have its way.

He stands over his daughter in the fading firelight. In the morning, the group will have to move on, and she will remain here, in this cave, where he will never see her again.

It's odd to him. His daughter is here, the same small body that gazes up at him with bright eyes. But something is gone. What has disappeared and made her cold and stiff?

He does not yet have a word to describe what happens when his spear strikes a beast in its heart, or when the elders slip away, but he is intimately familiar with it. The group must hunt for survival. He does not grieve when they bring down a beast and tear apart its flesh for meat and pelts. But this one does not feel right. She was too young to get so weak.

In the final days, when the group walked, he carried her. Typically a member so weak would be left behind, but this time the rest of the group allowed it. She was so light it did not slow him down.

She will never stand or run again, he knows. But in his head, she is still there, her gallop and curious eyes. How? Why? Where has she gone?

He does not like this feeling.

He pulls off the heavy pelt he has on and wraps it over his daughter's body. She is curled up within it, her eyes shut. If he had not touched her cold, hard flesh, he would have thought she was sleeping. The cave now is cold, especially as the fire turns to embers, but he does not shiver. He digs his fingers deep into the soil. The earth is unforgiving, breaking apart his nails and numbing his fingers, but he must do this.

The beast the pelt came from was ferocious. It gave him the deep scar on his shoulder that still aches on cold nights. It took three men to take the beast down, and it fed the group for several days.

He does not know where his daughter is going, but he does not want her to be alone.

- Malena McKaba

A Nobody's Will

I had been staring out towards the horizon for what felt like hours now, watching the dull, cloudy sky as it hid its light away, the old seagulls swooping down into the murky sea to catch their prey, the deafening horns of the port ships releasing their bouts of smoke, going about their daily routines. Everything about this area, town even, was never changing. I gripped the railings of the rusty bridge, wondering whether I should jump. I thought about how difficult it would be to swim to survival if I were to change my mind, what with my heavy, thick overcoat and all. My nieces would understand, right? That was rhetorical, they wouldn't. Nobody would. Nobody does. Not even their mother, who once upon a time I would've considered my lifeline. God knows what she's doing these days. And now, the only one in my life I might have given a similar title to would be the eager, grey squirrel, who I named Chipper on a whim, who comes to visit me often when I walk around the port, hoping for food. A couple weeks ago simply thinking about these meaningless things would have emotionally sent me off the edge. Like this very edge that my calloused hands can't seem to let go of, in fact. I've been holding on for hours. But now my tear ducts have all but run dry. Their salty streams stolen away by the sea, along with the old-fashioned mobile I once owned that I'd use in attempts to contact those I used to know, including my so-called lifeline, trying to reach anyone away from this depressing, poor excuse of a community. Lately the only thing that seems to make me smile is the thought of leaving it all behind. Not that there's much to leave behind. I have no partner, no offspring, and I hardly speak to my extended family, doubt they'd want to speak to me. To say my days are repetitive would be a colossal understatement. God how I wish they were numbered. Each morning I drag myself over to my shitty job, finish a long, underpaid shift of selling stale, expiring "goods" to the same locals every time, and then I come down to the port for the rest of the day because I'd rather gouge my eyes out than sit in my tiny abode while it's still daylight, my only company being the eerie silence that lingers on the east side of town and the cobwebs that surround the entire perimeter of the studio flat.

I let out a deep sigh in a futile attempt to clear my mind.

Earlier today, I noticed Chipper wasn't around. I pulled out my lighter and cigarette, idly thinking as I took my first puff, "Maybe he had a family to go back home to." I briefly thought about how other people of the town perceive me, recalling rumours of being called a loner, a creepy port dweller, bird-whisperer, etc. It almost made me chuckle, how none of it fazed me anymore. I blankly stared at the sea again as I took another puff, bringing my gaze slightly higher as I noticed how much the smoke resembled the heavy, grey clouds above me, followed it with my eyes as it kept floating up & up & up, as if returning to its home. I then looked over again at the same substance bellowing out from the cargo boats and it all made me ponder about if everything is connected and if lives, including mine, were meaningful. What a childish fantasy. I continued staring as the cheap ashes burned and my mind grew numb, leaning closer to the rails out of curiosity, although unfortunately I'm not a cat, and it was then that I sensed something. I was too in my own head to pick up much more than that but it felt like whatever I was sensing was invisibly all around me in the wind. It was ultimately pointless to try and figure it out because whatever it was, it was getting closer. I closed my eyes trying to ground myself but I felt as if my feet were no longer on solid pavement. I heard the cranking sounds of metal in the distance and then a voice. I felt the voice getting nearer and more demanding but it was too muffled for me to make out a word. I gasped as I felt my body lose all control of itself and I couldn't do anything. I smiled as I realised my life already felt like this constantly, every day. I concluded that whatever was happening was probably for the best and hoped I wouldn't have to worry or fret about anything again. The last thought on my mind was of my cigarette that I had watched return to the clouds, in a meaningless cycle that I'd finally be free from.

- Kassua Valente

Our Contributors

Nadia Arioli is the founder and editor in chief of *Thimble Literary Magazine*. A three-time Best of the Net and Pushcart Nominee, Arioli's poetry, artwork, and essays can be found in *Rust + Moth, Pithead Chapel, Hunger Mountain, Mom Egg Review, Permafrost*, and elsewhere. Arioli's latest collections are with Dancing Girl and Kelsay Books.

Amy Barone's poetry collection, "Defying Extinction," was published by Broadstone Books in 2022. New York Quarterly Books released her collection "We Became Summer," in 2018. Her poetry chapbooks include "Kamikaze Dance" (Finishing Line Press) and "Views from the Driveway" (Foothills Publishing.)

Walter Bargen has published 26 books of poetry including "My Other Mother's Red Mercedes" (Lamar University Press, 2018), "Until Next Time" (Singing Bone Press, 2019), and "Pole Dancing in the Night Club of God" (Red Mountain Press, 2020). In 2008, he was appointed the first poet laureate of Missouri.

Lawrence Bridges' poetry has appeared in *The New Yorker, Poetry, and The Tampa Review*. He has published three volumes of poetry: "Horses on Drums" (Red Hen Press, 2006), "Flip Days" (Red Hen Press, 2009), and "Brownwood" (Tupelo Press, 2016). You can find him on IG: @larrybridges

Kevin B is a writer from New England. Their work has appeared in *Apricity, Molecule, New Plains Review,* and *Havik*. They are the winner of the George Lila Award for Short Fiction, and the author of "Combustion."

Sam Brunk is the author of various works of history—including two books on Mexican revolutionary Emiliano Zapata. He has not previously published fiction, but his short story "Loach" received a prize in the Writer's Digest Short Short Story contest in 2023. "The Border" is adapted from his unpublished novel, "The Doctors Have Their Words."

Elise Chadwick taught English in Chappaqua, NY for 30 years. She lives in New York City but spends weekends in upstate NY, coexisting with the deer, groundhog, fox, bats, and rabbit who got there first. Her poems have been recently published in *The Paterson Literary Review, Healing Muse,* and *The English Journal.*

Alison Colwell's creative non-fiction work can be found in the climate-fiction anthology *Rising Tides, Folklife Magazine, The Fieldstone Review, the NonBinary Review,* and in *The Humber Literary Review.*

The bilingual child of American parents, **Johanna DeMay** grew up in Mexico City. Writing poems became her way to bridge the gap between her worlds. "Waypoints," a collection of her work, was released by Finishing Line Press in 2022.

Betty Dobson has been writing poetry and fiction for decades, and her portfolio is filled with published and prize-winning works. After taking a break from writing in recent years, she is now flexing her creative muscles once more.

A native of Ireland and a lapsed neurologist, **Ivo Drury** lives along the California Coast. Poetry published recently or pending publication featured in *Red Eft Review, Rockvale Review, Trouvaille Review,* and *Schuylkill Valley Journal* among others.

Benjamin Green is the author of eleven books including "The Sound of Fish Dreaming" (Bellowing Ark Press, 1996). At the age of sixty-seven, he hopes his new work articulates a mature vision of the world and does so with some integrity. He resides in Jemez Springs, New Mexico.

Jean Hackett lives in San Antonio and the Texas Hill Country. Her poetry has appeared in *Easing the Edges, Yellow Flag, No Season for Silence, FPL 2022 and 2023 Ekphrastic Poetry Anthologies, Purifying Wind, Plants and Poetry Journal, Voices de la Luna, The Langdon Review,* and *Arts Alive SA*. Her chapbook, "Masked/ Unmuted" was published in 2022.

Hossein Hakim has a Ph.D. in Electrical Engineering from Purdue University, West Lafayette, Indiana. His interests are philosophy, history, poetry, playing pickleball and traveling around the world. His poem "Cinema Paradiso" was accepted for publication in the August 2023 Issue of *Ariel Chart International Literary Journal*. In accepting this poem, Jana Begovic, Senior Editor of the Ariel Chart wrote to Hossein: "You definitely have a talent to tell moving stories in free verse."

Roger Hart's stories and essays have appeared in *Natural Bridge, The Tampa Review, Passages North, Runner's World,* and other magazines and journals. His stories have won the Marguerite McGlinn Prize, the Third Coast Fiction Prize, and the Dogwood Journal Fiction Prize. His most recent story collection, "Mysteries of the Universe," was published by Kallisto Gaia Press.

Corinne Hawk (she/they) is a queer writer, (dis)abled activist, and performance artist. Their work has appeared in *Bridge Eight Press, EroZine,* and *the zine Dear Social Workers*. She once found a note addressed from Diane di Prima to Starhawk wedged between the pages of a used copy of Loba. They keep the note from Diane framed above her desk in lieu of a degree. She lives – unhoused – in upstate New York.

Elizabeth Hill was a Finalist in the 2022 Rattle Poetry Contest, with the poem also appearing as Poem of the Day on February 20, 2023. She was nominated for the Pushcart Prize by the *Last Stanza Poetry Journal*. Her poetry has also been published in *34th Parallel Magazine, Blue Lake Review, SAND,* and *I-70 Review*, among other journals.

Don Hogle has published over ninety poems in almost sixty journals, including *Atlanta Review, Carolina Quarterly, Chautauqua, Hayden's Ferry Review,* and *The Ocotillo Review*. He was a finalist for the 2023 Tucson Festival of Books Literary Awards. His debut chapbook, "Madagascar," was published in 2020 by Sevens Kitchens Press. He lives in Manhattan. www.donhoglepoet.com

Jennifer Hu is a Taiwanese-American writer based in San Francisco. Her work has received support from VONA, Kenyon Review Writers Workshop, and the National Foundation for the Advancement of Artists. As an active member of the Bay Area literary community, she has read her work at Lit Quake and the Bay Area Book Festival. She is working on her first novel about food, art, and old family secrets.

Dorothy Johnson-Laird is a poet and social worker who lives in New York City. She has a passion for African music and has published music journalism with www.worldmusiccentral.org. Recent poems appeared in *Cantos* and *Pedestal Magazine*, among others.

Darryl Lauster is an Intermedia artist, writer, and an Associate Chair of the Art and Art History Department at the University of Texas Arlington. His writing has been published by *Gulf Coast Magazine, Art Lies Magazine, North by Northeast, Crack the Spine, The Conversation, The Athenaeum Review,* and *The CAA Art Journal*. His first novel, "Rites of Passage," was published by Creators Publishing in 2017.

Dotty Le Mieux's latest chapbook—"Viruses, Guns and War"—was published this year by Main Street Rag Press. She has published in numerous publications including *Rise Up Review, Sheila Na-Gig, Writers Resist,* and *Gyroscope,* and has four previous chapbooks.

E. D. Lloyd-Kimbrel, whose car masquerades as a branch library, over time has published biographical, critical, and scholarly essays, creative non-fiction, and poetry.

Linda Zamora Lucero's stories have been published in *Somos En Escrito, LatineLit, Cutthroat, Yellow Medicine, Puro Chicanx Writers of the 21st Century,* and *Bilingual Review*. She is a Pushcart nominee, and her story "Speak to Me of Love," was awarded first prize in the DeMarinis Short Story Contest.

Kurt Luchs (kurtluchs.com) is a Contributing Editor of *Exacting Clam*, and won a 2022 Pushcart Prize and a 2021 James Tate Poetry Prize. His humor collection, "It's Funny Until Someone Loses an Eye

(Then It's Really Funny)" (2017), and his poetry collection, "Falling in the Direction of Up" (2021), are published by Sagging Meniscus Press. His latest poetry chapbook is "The Sound of One Hand Slapping" (2022) from SurVision Books (Dublin, Ireland).

The poetry of **Richard Lyons** has appeared in *Poetry, The New Republic,* and *The Paris Review*. His fourth book of poems, "Un Poco Loco" from Iris Books was published in 2016. He is the author of two chapbooks of poems: "Heart House" in 2019, and "Sleep on Needles" in 2023.

Jenny Maaketo (she/her) is a neurodivergent poet from Austin, Texas. She is a first-year candidate in the MFA Creative Writing program at the University of Mississippi. Jenny was shortlisted in the 2023 Crab Creek Review Poetry Prize, the 2023 Michelle Boisseau Poetry Prize, and the 2022 Patty Friedmann Writing Competition. Her poems appear or are forthcoming in *The Crab Creek Review, The Cordite Poetry Review,* and *The Madison Review* among others.

Malena McKaba is currently the fiction editor at *Two Headed Press*. Previously, her work has appeared in *Chinquapin* and *Red Wheelbarrow Anthology*, and short films that she's directed have shown at film festivals across the country. Malena is currently lingering in Oakland, California, with her tabby cat.

Eva Nemirovsky (they/she) received a bachelors in English from the University of California, Davis, before moving to a one-semester mentorship program with Gayle Brandeis at the PocketMFA online workshop. They've published poetry in *The Ocotillo Review*, and prose in *The Pomona Valley Review*. When they aren't writing, they're rock climbing, drawing, or spending time with their cat, Apollo, in their home in Davis.

Karl Plank's poetry has appeared in journals such as *Beloit Poetry Journal, Zone 3,* and *Tahoma Literary Review*, and has been featured on Poetry Daily. He is the Cannon Professor of Religion, Emeritus, at Davidson College.

Kirie Pedersen's writing appears in *New Orleans Review, Rumpus, Hunger Mountain, Emrys Journal, Miracle Monocle, Superstition Review, Cleaver, Still Point Arts Quarterly, PANK,* and elsewhere, and includes nominations for Pushcarts, Best American Essays, and other awards. "Getting a Life" was selected as Notable for Best American Essays. Additional writing appears at http://www.kiriepedersen.com. Please check out Kirie's Artist Chicken newsletter on Substack.

Jennifer M Phillips is a bi-national immigrant, painter, gardener, Bonsai-grower. Her chapbooks: "Sitting Safe In the Theatre of Electricity" (i-blurb.com, 2020) and "A Song of Ascents" (Orchard Street Press, 2022). A poem is like a little brass pan to carry fire's coals through the winter weather, and so she writes.

Michael Salcman is the former chairman of neurosurgery at the University of Maryland, a child of the Holocaust, and survivor of polio. Poems in *Barrow Street, Harvard Review, Hopkins Review, Hudson Review* and *Smartish Pace*. Books include "The Clock Made of Confetti," "Poetry in Medicine, classic and contemporary poems on medicine," "A Prague Spring" (Sinclair Poetry Prize), "Shades & Graces," Daniel Hoffman Legacy Book Prize winner, and "Necessary Speech: New & Selected Poems" (Spuyten Duyvil in 2022).

Rikki Santer's poems have appeared in various publications including *Poetry East, Heavy Feather Review, Slab, Slipstream, [PANK], Crab Orchard Review, RHINO, Grimm, Hotel Amerika* and *The Main Street Rag*. Her work has received many honors including Pushcart, Ohioana and Ohio Poet book award nominations, a fellowship from the National Endowment for the Humanities. Her twelfth poetry collection, "Resurrection Letter: Leonora, Her Tarot, and Me," is a sequence in tribute to the surrealist artist Leonora Carrington.

Jacqueline Schaalje has published poetry and short fiction, most recently in *The Comstock Review, The Friday Poem, and Pembroke Magazine*. She's the winner of the Florida Review Editor's Prize 2022. She is a translation editor at *MAYDAY* Magazine.

Claire Scott is an award-winning poet who has received multiple Pushcart Prize nominations. Her work has appeared in *The Atlanta Review, Bellevue Literary Review, New Ohio Review* and *Healing Muse* among others.

Hilary Sideris is the author of "Un Amore Veloce" (Kelsay Books 2019), "The Silent B" (Dos Madres Press 2019), "Animals in English, poems after Temple Grandin" (Dos Madres Press 2020), and "Liberty Laundry" (Dos Madres Press 2022.)

Valerie A. Smith's debut, "Back to Alabama," is forthcoming from Sundress Publications. She has a PhD from Georgia State and a MA from Kennesaw State, where she currently teaches English. Her poems appear in *Radix, Aunt Chloe, Weber, Spectrum, Obsidian, Crosswinds, Dogwood, Solstice, Oyster River Pages,* and *Wayne Literary Review.*

Roz Spafford grew up on a cattle ranch in Arizona, where much of her work is set. She now teaches writing in Toronto.

Danny Spatchek was born and raised in rural Wisconsin. A high school English teacher in South Korea for the past 10 years, he has work forthcoming in the literary journals *Seems* and *Great Lakes Review.*

Jeff Stone gave up a capitalist corpo career during the pandemic to write full-time. Years from now, many may call him a fool for doing so, but alas, that will be years from now. He resides among the Blue Ridge Mountains and aside from 25+ years of writing ad copy, he is a newly published (*Heimat Review, Intrepidus Ink, Backwards Trajectory, Invisible City*) writer of stories of whatever length they demand of him.

Kassua Valente is a young, upcoming writer from London with experience in writing reviews, fanfiction, flash fiction and a poem or two. Her hobbies include gushing about the latest animes on air, journaling about life and noting down ideas for the next piece. Her biggest fan is her English tutor Sally, who inspired her to take a dive into the world of literature, and she hasn't looked back since.

Catherine Vance is an interfaith chaplain whose novel "The Mountains Under Her Feet" was published in March 2023. A winner of the Dobie-Paisano Award from the Texas Institute of Letters, she holds an MFA from Washington University in St. Louis and is currently completing an MDiv at Iliff School of Theology in Denver. Her work has appeared in *Memoir Magazine, Herstory, Wraparound South, Defunkt Magazine, Talking Writing, Asylum, Synkroniciti, Visible Magazine*, and elsewhere.

Bonnie Wehle is a docent at the University of Arizona Poetry Center and facilitates a monthly poetry circle via Zoom. Her work has appeared in *Coal Hill Review, Rockvale Review, River Heron Review, Sky Islands Journal*, and elsewhere. Her chapbook, "A Certain Ache: Poems in Women's Voices," was released by Finishing Line Press in 2022.

Jamie Wendt is the author of the poetry collection "Fruit of the Earth" (Main Street Rag, 2018). Her manuscript, "Laughing in Yiddish," was a finalist for the 2022 Philip Levine Prize in Poetry. Her poems have been published in various literary journals and anthologies, including *Catamaran, Green Mountains Review, Lilith, Jet Fuel Review, Poetica Magazine*, and others. She contributes book reviews to the Jewish Book Council. She lives and teaches in Chicago.

Sean Whalen is a retiring health and safety professional from central Iowa. His poems have appeared in multiple publications, including *Flyway, Grasslands Review, The Mid-America Poetry Review, Mid-American Review, Plainsongs, Halcyon Days, Founder's Favorites*, and *Last Leaves*, and are forthcoming in *Smoky Blue* and *After Happy Hour*.

Yance Wyatt is a hearing-impaired author from rural Tennessee. He received an MFA from USC before becoming a writing professor there. A two-time Pushcart Prize nominee, his work is published or forthcoming in *Zyzzyva, THEMA, The Los Angeles Review, The Northwest Review*, and *The Pinch*.

Edward Ziegler lives and writes in the Wildcat Mountains just South of Denver, Colorado. He is a native Kentuckian, a former All-American high school and Notre Dame footballer, and an Emeritus Professor of Law at the University of Denver. His personal essays and poetry are found in numerous literary reviews and he has been nominated for a Pushcart Prize. Online: edwardziegler.com

Coming in 2024
From Kallisto Gaia Press
Winner of the 2023 Saguaro Poetry Prize

Hunger House
by Jessica Turcat

Hunger House by Jessica Turcat explores the demands and promises of mortality as an observation. The midwestern rural voice of the collection establishes in minute detail the role of being alone in loneliness and finding the feminine in feminist. Turcat opens a frosted window for the unsung women who populate and moderate the flyover states only to find it is a mirror.

Printed in the USA
CPSIA information can be obtained
at www.ICGtesting.com
LVHW020026020324
773348LV00004B/539